Lily F. Wesselhoeft, J. F. Goodridge

Old Rough the Miser

A Fable for Children

Lily F. Wesselhoeft, J. F. Goodridge

Old Rough the Miser
A Fable for Children

ISBN/EAN: 9783744767569

Printed in Europe, USA, Canada, Australia, Japan

Cover: Foto ©Andreas Hilbeck / pixelio.de

More available books at **www.hansebooks.com**

" And, with a few prodigious leaps, gained the stream, into which she sprang."

PAGE 273.

OLD ROUGH THE MISER.

A Fable for Children.

BY

LILY F. WESSELHOEFT,

AUTHOR OF "SPARROW THE TRAMP," "FLIPWING THE SPY," "THE WINDS,
THE WOODS, AND THE WANDERER."

ILLUSTRATED BY J. F. GOODRIDGE.

BOSTON:
ROBERTS BROTHERS.
1891.

UNIVERSITY PRESS:
JOHN WILSON AND SON, CAMBRIDGE, U.S.A.

CONTENTS.

"At last, bleeding and maimed, they agreed to lay the case before the owl."

CHAPTER I.

THE BEGINNING OF THE FEUD.

ONCE upon a time there lived on a large farm a crow, a water-rat, an owl, a frog, and a weasel. Large as the farm was, with its meadows, its fields, and many acres of woodland, it would seem as if these little animals might have lived in harmony, without encroaching on one another's domains. Such was not the case, however; and indeed it is a well-known fact that the more one has the more one wants, and that there are some who wish to possess the earth.

This is how the quarrel began. The water-rat, who lived on the edge of the brook, claimed the right to a cornfield near by, which the crow had always considered his own. The quarrel ended in a fierce fight which lasted many hours, neither being able to conquer the other. At last, bleeding and maimed, they agreed to lay the case before the owl and abide by his decision, for he had the reputation of being very wise.

One moonlight night, the owl repaired to a large oak-tree on the edge of the wood; and about him assembled the crow and the water-rat, with various friends whom they had brought as witnesses, besides many other interested parties.

Very solemn did Judge Owl look, as he sat with his great yellow eyes wide open and staring straight before him. The trial was conducted with great formality, each party stating his own case.

First the crow called up his witnesses, field-mice and squirrels. All expressed the opinion that the cornfield belonged by right to the crow, because they had been told by their fathers and grandfathers that the crows had always held possession of it.

After this testimony, the water-rat stated *his* case, and summoned *his* witnesses the frogs. They were of opinion that the water-rat should have the cornfield because he had always had it, and because he could n't live on the food the brook afforded him. Much bickering went on between the witnesses of both parties, until Judge Owl interposed thus, —

"Come to order, and pay attention to what I say. I have heard both sides, and my mind is made up. The cornfield belongs to the crow."

Angry squeals were heard from the water-rat, and loud croaks of disapproval from his witnesses the frogs, who sided with him,— not from a conviction that he was right, but because he held control of the brook and threatened to keep them out of it unless they testified in his favor.

"Silence!" commanded the judge, with an angry hoot. "The cornfield, I say, belongs to the crow, for corn is his natural food. What business has a water-rat with corn? None at all. I am told it is indigestible for him; and all I can say is, that if it *does* agree with him it ought not to, and that it is a mistake. The brook is the place for the water-rat: let him stay there, and live on what he can find in it. If he can't find anything, let him go without it,—that is his look-out. Can crows live in the water? No. Consequently the cornfield belongs by right to the crow.

"Another argument in favor of the crow is that he can fly off when anybody comes. Can a water-rat fly? Not that I ever heard of. There is still another argument, and one that is indisputable. Was there ever a cornfield that did n't have a scare-crow in it? Did anybody ever hear of a scare-*rat?* General opinion carries the day, — the corn-field belongs to the crow.

"Now I command you to keep the peace. As long as the water-rat persists in his absurd claims, there will be bloodshed and strife. I will repeat to you a verse from 'The Laws of the Woods,' that states the case as clearly as daylight — I should say moonlight.

> "' War and strife, grief and woe,
> Follow you where'er you go.
> Never more shall you know rest
> For weary feet and aching breast,

> Till body round and lithe and long
> Shall vanquish body thick and strong.
> Then shall dawn a day of peace,
> And every strife and sorrow cease.'

"Now the matter is settled, and I must be off, as I have another case to decide on the farther side of the wood;" and away flew Judge Owl.

Exulting caws from the victorious crow and triumphant squeaks from the mice followed; but with an angry squeal the water-rat announced his determination to keep possession of the cornfield. The verse from the "Laws of the Woods" that the judge had read, had no meaning for the assembled party; nor indeed had it for the judge himself, who had pondered long over it, and perhaps this had something to do with his hasty departure.

Consequently, the decision of the owl did not change matters in the least, — both the crow and the water-rat claimed the cornfield as before. The mice and squirrels sided with the crow, and the frogs with the water-rat ; and the water-rat hated the crow even more than before, and vowed vengeance on the mice and squirrels for taking part against him.

The weasel, like the owl, had no especial interest in the matter at stake, but kept by himself, living under stone walls or in the neighborhood of hen-roosts and barns, — a deadly enemy of rats and mice, and consequently carefully avoided by them.

In this manner things went on until our story opens, several generations later. The scene of action is the same farm, but the originators of the quarrel have been long dead and forgotten, having transmitted the feud to their descendants.

"He soon reached the opening, before which stood a little field-
mouse, who glanced timidly up."

CHAPTER II.

OLD ROUGH AT HOME.

OUR story opens on a dark day in summer, and in a piece of woodland so far
removed from the busy life that stirs cities

and large villages, that it was seldom any sound arose to break the stillness of Nature, except those made by the animal creation who dwelt there undisturbed by the depredations of mankind.

At a first glance, it would seem as if not even animal life were there, so profound was the silence. A brook, or more properly a ditch, for so sluggish a stream hardly deserved the name of a brook, flowed torpidly through a meadow which was bordered by forest trees and thickly growing underbrush.

At a first glance, as we said, no motion was perceptible, but a keen eye on the lookout for signs of life might have detected a dark object creeping along the soft and slimy banks of the ditch, often stopping to look about him and listen. It was a large water-rat, his long rough fur failing to make him an agreeable object, for the cruel expression in his keen little eyes that were placed closely together, and the long, sharp teeth that seemed constantly on the look-out for something to devour, would have deformed any face.

As the water-rat proceeded cautiously on his way, as we said before, he stopped frequently and looked about him, sometimes casting his sharp eyes around to see if anybody were approaching, and at all times on the watch for trespassers on his domains; for the water-rat considered himself the proprietor of the meadow, and in a measure also of the forest that stretched beyond it.

All at once, the old rat stopped short and examined the ground about him, where the prints of small feet in the mud were visible. "I thought so!" he exclaimed to himself; "those mischievous field-mice have been here again, gnawing those tender young roots that I have been keeping my eye on. Just let me catch them at it, and their tails will be even shorter than they are now.

They're even worse than the crows, for they are so small they can slink around without being seen."

A jeering laugh from behind startled the water-rat, and turning quickly he descried two young crows seated on a rock near by, and regarding him with countenances expressive of great amusement.

" Be off, you young thieves," snarled the old rat, angrily ; " how dare you trespass on my premises ? "

For answer the young crows each inclined an ear toward the water-rat in a listening attitude, as if to catch his words, and then burst into derisive caws.

"Don't speak quite so loudly, sir," remarked one of the crows. " I knew an old fellow of about your age who busted a blood-vessel, and 't would be a pity to have you taken off so suddenly; you'd be a great loss to the neighborhood, you're so sociable."

"And he was first cousin to the fellow who died because he tried to save expense by living without eating," said the other crow.

The old water-rat was too wise to continue a conversation in which he was sure to be worsted; so he continued on his way, followed by the taunts of the young crows.

"How much will you take for your skin, old Rough?" called out one, while the other chanted,—

> "There was once an old miser, who thought
> He could live upon little or nought;
> But one day he died,
> And his wife sold his hide
> For a sum much more than she ought."

"Young villains!" muttered old Rough to himself, as he scurried home, "I'll pay them for this."

The water-rat stopped before a hole, and looking stealthily behind him, to make sure that no one was in sight, noiselessly entered his habitation.   A long and narrow passage, in which the darkness increased as he progressed, led finally into a large apartment, which served evidently as the living and sleeping room of old Rough; for a pile of dried leaves and old rags in one corner apparently served as a bed.

Another rat sat on this bed, evidently in the act of taking a hasty lunch, for so silent had been her husband's entrance that Ruffina was not aware of his approach until he appeared before her; then with a frightened expression she hastily swallowed the mouthful she was masticating, and with a quick motion concealed something under the leaves that formed the bed.

"Not so fast, madam," exclaimed old Rough, springing to the spot where his wife had hidden her prize; and in a twinkling he drew forth a large walnut, into which Ruffina had had time only to drill a hole with her sharp teeth.

"So, madam!" exclaimed the old rat in a

harsh voice, looking from the nut to his trembling wife, whose eyes anxiously followed all his movements, " so this is the way you obey me, is it ?   How dared you touch those nuts when you knew they were not to be eaten ? "

" But they are last year's nuts, and most of them are wormy and musty," answered Ruffina, submissively ; " and I thought you would n't care."

" You thought I would n't care ? " squealed the old rat, bringing his teeth together with a snap that made his wife shiver.

" I was so hungry," pleaded Ruffina, meekly, " and the nuts are really spoiled."

" What ! " shrieked old Rough, with a spring that brought him in front of his terrified wife, " have you lost the little sense you ever possessed ? Don't you know that I can mix those nuts in with this year's, and pass them off for fresh ones ? And see here, madam, I think you said just now that you were hungry. Don't let me hear any more of such nonsense. Don't you eat as much as I do? We must pinch and scrape, and *starve* if necessary, to get a little forehanded, or we shall die paupers."

"But we are not poor," replied Ruffina, meekly. "Look at the piles of roots and mussels and snails over there. Every one says you are richer than anybody about here, and —"

Poor Ruffina ended her sentence in a cry of pain, for her cruel husband darted suddenly upon her and fastened his long teeth in one of her ears.

"If you are too stupid to comprehend my words, perhaps you can understand that!" exclaimed the ill-natured old miser, as his poor wife retreated to a corner, whining.

A soft voice at the door here attracted old Rough's attention, and entering the passage-way, he soon reached the opening, before which stood a little field-mouse, who glanced timidly up at the hard face of the old miser.

"Well, what do you want, Bobtilla?" asked the old rat, with a grim smile at the discomfiture of the little field-mouse.

"I came to ask if I might have one of those tender roots down by the dam?" said Bobtilla, timidly.

"What!" exclaimed old Rough, harshly, "you have the audacity to ask me for one of my tender young roots?"

"One of my children is ill," squeaked Bobtilla in her mild voice, "and he thought he would relish one of them. He has so little appetite now that he can't eat the scraps I manage to pick up."

"Oh, he can't!" growled the old rat. "Well, what will you give me in exchange for my tender young root? Do you know, madam, that every one of those little roots brings me a pile of corn?"

"I shall without doubt be able to pay

you when the crops are ripe," answered the little field-mouse; "but we have eaten up all our winter store, and shall have to scrape along as best we can till midsummer."

"The more fool you," snarled the old water-rat. "Let me tell you, madam, that I don't indulge in luxuries; if I did, I should probably have to go about begging as you do. No, when you come with your pile of corn, you shall have the tender root that your sick child craves, not before. Now be off. You 're a thieving set, like all the others about here, and I want you to keep off my premises;" and the old miser turned and re-entered his dwelling.

Poor little Bobtilla turned sorrowfully away from the miser's abode, and retraced her steps to her home. How could she go back to her sick child and tell him that she had returned without the tender root he so much desired? The more Bobtilla thought over the matter, the harder it seemed to her, and she cast many a longing glance toward the dam where the tender roots grew.

"Why did the miser claim the whole meadow?" thought Bobtilla. He had no more right to it than she or many others. Merely by right of his superior strength did he claim it. Was it possible she could gnaw off a small piece without being detected? Bobtilla hesitated as she arrived opposite the dam, and glanced quickly in the direction of the tyrant's abode. Far off as it was, she was certain she saw the miser sitting in the doorway, and trembling at the thought of the terrible revenge that would overtake her should she attempt to touch the coveted root, she reluctantly continued her way.

As Bobtilla passed under the wall that led to her home, pleasant tones fell on her ear, and the voice being a new one, she stopped and looked about her. A chipmunk whom she had never before seen, sat on the top of the wall, holding in her little forepaws a large nut, into which she was drilling a hole, at the same time conversing in a cheerful voice with another chipmunk, who sat on the branch of a large chestnut-tree above her. Bobtilla, hidden behind a stone, paused to listen.

"So he told you they were his trees, and that we could n't have any of the nuts when they were ripe, did he?" said the squirrel on the wall, examining the nut to see how deep the hole had become.

"Yes, my dear," replied the squirrel on the tree; "but I reminded him that the wood was a large place, and that there was room for all in it."

"What did he say to that?" asked the other squirrel, whose sharp teeth had now penetrated the hard shell of the nut.

"Oh! he still kept up his bluster; but I think we need n't fear him. I don't know who he is, that he should give himself so many airs, but we can let him alone, and perhaps he will not interfere with us."

"I can tell you who he is," squeaked Bobtilla; "he is a disagreeable old miser, and his name is old Rough."

The two squirrels looked about them in astonishment, for they had thought themselves alone, and the little field-mouse hopped onto the stone behind which she had been concealed.

"I can tell you all about him," she said. "You must be strangers about here not to know who old Rough is. I was at his house just now, to beg a little root of him. There are ever so many of them growing down by the dam, and I thought he might let me have one for my sick child; but he refused, because I had no corn to give him in exchange. You see our winter supply has gone," continued Bobtilla, who was encouraged to proceed by the good-natured countenances of her listeners, "and one of my children is ill, and can't eat as the rest of us do. All we had was a grasshopper's leg that was hard and dry. It is of no use to try to soften old Rough's heart, and I suppose I must see my child die for want of proper food."

The two squirrels exchanged glances, and the mother squirrel, Squirrella, said,—

"Would your sick child relish a nut, do you think? I am quite sure we have a few chestnuts left, and they are quite easy to break;" and before Bobtilla could reply, Squirrella had disappeared in a hole in the wall. In an instant she was back again, carrying a chestnut in her mouth; and depositing it at the feet of the little field-mouse, she said in her motherly way,—

"When he has eaten that come back for more. I know what it is to have sick children.

"We have but just moved here," continued Squirrella, interrupting Bobtilla's profuse thanks. "We have always lived in one place, but the woods were being thinned out to make room for human habitations, and we felt the necessity for a change. One day our friend Swift the swallow told us of this place, so we moved here."

"This seems a very peaceful place," said Squirrello, the squirrel on the tree, "and I don't see how old Rough can hurt us if we keep out of his way. All of your other neighbors are harmless, are n't they?"

"Yes," replied Bobtilla, "I believe so,— unless it is old Blinkeye. He is very strong and fierce, you know, — that is at night. Nobody is afraid of him in the daytime, for then he can't see a thing."

"Old Blinkeye, — and what kind of a creature is he?" asked Squirrello.

"A very large owl," replied the field-mouse. "As I said before, look out for him at night, for then he is dangerous; but in the daytime, why he could n't harm a fly, and I would n't even turn out of the way if I met him."

Here a slight rustling of the leaves in a tall tree near by attracted their attention, and, giving one hurried glance in that direction, Bobtilla shrieked, " Old Blinkeye !" and in spite of her assertion that he was perfectly harmless in the daytime, seized her chestnut, and darted off to her home with great speed, not once stopping to look behind her.

The two squirrels, startled by Bobtilla's sudden exclamation, took the alarm, and whisked into their hole in the wall.

" Well, young gentlemen, he began in the high, cracked voice of
extreme age, you did well to return."

CHAPTER III.

OLD CAW'S COUNSEL.

WHEN the two chipmunks found themselves inside their house, they listened
in breathless silence, their little hearts beat-

ing fast with fear; but as all was still, and they found they were not pursued, curiosity began to get the better of them, and they felt a desire to obtain a glimpse of the dangerous being that had inspired Bobtilla with such terror.

Noiselessly approaching the opening of their house, Squirrello put out his head and glanced cautiously around. On the tall tree sat a large bird, such as the squirrel, who had hitherto lived on the outskirts of a large town, had never seen. His strong claws grasped tightly the bough on which he rested, and his large yellow eyes that gleamed through the foliage looked straight before him. The pointed tufts on his head and his large hooked beak gave him a vigilant and fierce expression, and at intervals he blinked his eyes solemnly. It was a great grandson of Judge Owl, who, many years before, had settled the dispute between the crow and the water-rat.

Squirrello having made these observations from his door, turned and addressed his wife, —

"Come, Squirrella, and look at this strange creature. We have certainly seen nothing like him."

Squirrella glanced toward a corner of her house, where, on a soft bed of leaves and moss, lay two young chipmunks fast asleep.

"They are all right," replied her husband, reassuringly, "old Blinkeye can't get in here."

"How I dread the time when they are old enough to run about by themselves," said Squirrella, anxiously. "I almost wish we had remained where we were."

"You forget the cats there," answered her husband. "Evidently old Blinkeye is the only creature we need fear besides the water-rat, and owls are dangerous only at night."

"Then why did the field-mouse seem so alarmed at sight of him?" asked Squirrella.

"Because she is afraid of everything. Come, my dear, don't be as foolish as she is, but take a good look at this remarkable-looking bird, that you may avoid him in future."

Thus encouraged, Squirrella took heart and followed her husband to the door, and after a moment, seeing how silently and quietly the owl sat on his perch, she became emboldened to join her husband on the top of the wall, where they both remained, watching the great solemn eyes of the fierce Blinkeye.

The two chipmunks conversed in low tones, and the owl was evidently not aware of their presence, for he still looked straight before him in the same solemn manner.

A laughing and cawing was heard before long, and two noisy young crows lighted on a tree directly opposite the silent owl.

"How are you, father Blinkeye?" asked one of the crows, familiarly. The owl turned his head slightly towards the voice, but maintained the same dignified silence.

"You don't happen to know what the parrot died of, do you, my friend?" asked the other crow; but as he received no answer, he continued, —

"Well, he died of talking, and I thought perhaps you might have symptoms of the same disease."

The owl continued silent as before, and fixed his solemn yellow eyes on the impertinent young crows, who after a while became somewhat uneasy under his steadfast gaze. With a show of indifference they indulged in personal remarks intended to annoy the silent owl, but to all their impertinence the owl was apparently unmoved, and at last broke silence: —

"Let me advise you, my young friends, for you are *very* young in experience, to be a little more careful in your selection of a place to conceal your stolen treasures. I am astonished that such shrewd young fellows as you consider yourselves should have shown so little judgment."

"What do you mean?" asked both together.

"Oh! nothing," answered the owl, carelessly. "I thought perhaps you might sometime have occasion to conceal a bone or delicate scrap of meat your old grandfather had given you as a reward for good behavior, and I have *heard* that you were not as careful as you might be in your selection of hiding-places."

"So you have been spying, have you?" exclaimed the younger crow, angrily.

"I?" asked the owl, coolly. "Oh, no, I was merely repeating what I had heard. Old bones and scraps of meat do not attract me; I prefer *live* game." And at the words, the two little chipmunks suddenly darted into their house, and remained there until the mischievous crows had taken flight, and all was still once more.

"You see, my young friends," continued the owl, "that you are better known than you think you are. Did you ever hear that verse about your family in 'The Laws of the Woods?' I will repeat it to you, that you may form some idea of the reputation you bear : —

> "' Wherever you are, and wherever you go,
> Beware, oh beware, of the saucy crow!
> His feathers are black and his beak is long,
> And he has a croak instead of a song.
> His pleasure it is to hide and to steal ;
> No creature for him does affection feel ;
> I pray you avoid him, the mischievous crow,
> For there 's no trick that he does not know.' "

"Capital!" exclaimed the two crows, bursting into caws of laughter. "Give us some more verses from 'The Laws of the Woods'!"

"I will," replied the owl, severely, and still gazing fixedly on them, he repeated in warning notes : —

> " ' War and strife, grief and woe,
>   Follow you where'er you go.
>   Never more shall you know rest
>   For weary feet and aching breast,
>   Till body round and lithe and long
>   Shall vanquish body thick and strong.
>   Then shall dawn a day of peace,
>   And every strife and sorrow cease.' "

" Suppose you tell us what it means ? " said the elder crow. " Who is the ' body round and lithe and long,' and who the ' body thick and strong' ? "

" You will find out to your sorrow before long," replied the owl, solemnly; " but ' the day of peace ' will dawn for the rest of us."

" In return for your compliment, I 'll recite for your benefit a verse that is a little easier to understand," said the elder crow : —

> " There was once an owl who said, ' I
>   Really would not hurt a fly; '
>   And through the long day,
>   He sat blinking away,
>   But when the night came, oh my ! "

As the crow finished his verse, he and his brother flew off with great flapping of wings and derisive jeers, cawing out the lines as long as they were within hearing of the owl.

When they were out of sight, the two crows looked at each other, and the younger said, —

"How do you suppose he found out about that pig's ear?"

"I'm sure I don't know; somebody probably watched us. One thing he said is true, — he always wants live food himself."

"I'll tell you how it is," replied the younger brother, "Old Rough is an acquaintance of his, and he is always prying about, and wouldn't hesitate to help himself to anything he might find. Yes, we'll have to find a new hiding-place."

"Hush!" said the elder brother, as they came in sight of their home; "don't talk so loudly. There's the old gentleman on the lookout, and old as he is, he hears quicker than any of us."

On the top of a tall fir-tree, where the branches grew thickest, reposed the home of the crow family,—and a most untidy and insecure structure it was, looking as if the materials had been flung against the tree and caught there; for mud and twigs, and rags and feathers appeared to be mixed indiscriminately, and the whole nest looked as though it might tumble down at any moment.

In spite, however, of the insecure appearance of her home, the mother crow was seated comfortably within, and several young crows were perched on neighboring branches, noisily cawing.

On a tree near by, apart from the others, as if he wished to avoid their noisy cawing, sat a crow whose appearance indicated that he was a person of distinction in the crow family, and when the hilarity of the younger crows grew unusually loud, the mother sitting in the nest glanced uneasily towards this solitary figure, and sharply enjoined silence.

For awhile after her admonitions, the voices became lower; but soon, with the exuberant spirits of youth, the young crows again forgot themselves, and they all cawed together as excitedly as before.

As the two newcomers appeared, the old crow on the tree by himself, turning his head sideways, glanced at them out of one eye, but otherwise bestowed no attention on them.

"Where have you been all day?" asked the mother crow in a querulous voice. "Your father has been everywhere to hunt for you, and your grandfather is much displeased."

"We were looking for provisions for the family," replied the elder brother, winking at the other.

"A likely story!" replied his mother. "You have been idling away your time in some folly, I know. You never *are* here when you 're wanted."

The young crows knew by experience that this was the beginning of a long lecture, and they remained silent until their mother had ended. All this time the old crow had not stirred; but when the mother bird had ceased, he said briefly,—

" Come here, I have something to say to you."

Their mother's scoldings the young crows did not mind, for they were too frequent to make a deep impression, and she told them of so many faults at once that her reproofs lost their force; but when old Caw their grandfather spoke, it was always to the point, and left them in no doubt as to his meaning.

The two young crows at once, therefore, obeyed the summons, and lighted on a branch opposite the old crow, who for a moment regarded them in silence. It was no wonder that the countenances of these reckless young creatures fell beneath the gaze of that shrewd old face.

Old Caw, as he was familiarly called, the leader of the flock, although having long outlived his generation of crows, had still sufficient energy of character left to enable him to sustain the position of counsellor and leader that he had for so many years ably borne. One eye only remained to him, the other having been pecked out in a quarrel in his youth; but in that single eye was concentrated all the shrewdness and ability that distinguished him even among the ablest of his kind.

" Well, young gentlemen," he began, in the high cracked voice of extreme old age, " you did well to return when you did. The expedition starts shortly, for we must have two good hours before sunset."

The young crows knew that it was not to tell them this that their grandfather had called them and eyed them so sharply, and they looked at one another sheepishly. As he continued silent, they turned to leave him; but he called them back.

"See here, my fine fellows, the next time you steal a pig's ear from me, don't be so clumsy about it. There is a right and wrong way of doing things, and you can't be too particular about these little matters."

The young crows looked still more confused, as they learned that their grandfather had discovered their little theft.

"Did you really think old Caw was so stupid as to hide his pig's ear where you could find it so easily? No, I assure you he is too old a head for that. I purposely put it where you would come upon it, for I wanted to teach you a lesson, and sometime I will show you how to do such things neatly. Your education has really been neglected. However, it is time to be off, and here come our friends."

As he spoke, several crows appeared, flying rapidly towards them. Very little time was spent in preparations for starting, and when all were in their places, old Caw placed himself at the head of the little flock, and with much flapping of wings and discordant cawing, they flew off in the direction of the woods.

"Many a smaller bird started up in terror from its leafy retreat, and occasionally a squirrel or rabbit scurried into its hole."

CHAPTER IV.

THE CORNFIELD.

OLD Caw led his flock of crows through the dense wood, and startled by the constant cawing that broke the stillness of the forest, many a smaller bird started up in terror from its leafy retreat, and occasionally a squirrel or rabbit scurried into its hole, to remain there with fast-beating hearts until the harsh noises had died away in the distance.

As they passed over a grove of pine-trees, they met another flock of crows flying in an opposite direction, and a discordant cawing arose from both parties, the elder members of each band trying, with the wisdom that age brings, to silence the younger ones; but in this attempt they were unsuccessful, and, with a few sharp words of reprimand, old Caw started his party again, with the exception of his two pugnacious grandsons, who remained behind to settle the dispute with two equally persistent members of the opposing party. Before long, however, they were seen rapidly flying to join their flock, in high spirits at having settled the matter to their satisfaction.

No other incident occurred to disturb the progress of old Caw's little band, and soon they passed over cultivated fields and open meadows, the keen eye of the veteran leader taking in all the possibilities of the country.

At last Caw halted his band on the edge of a fine maple grove, and they beheld before them a fertile field in which were planted crops of various kinds. It was the very cornfield about which, years before, the quarrel had arisen between the crow and the water-rat.

A stone wall, with a row of maple-trees in front of it, separated the field from the road.

"Why not light on those maple-trees, where we can see something going on, instead of hiding here in this out-of-the-way place?" asked one of the party.

"This is not Sunday," replied old Caw, severely.

"What has that to do with it?" asked a youthful member of the flock, while the one who had made the proposition retired abashed to the rear.

"What has that to do with it?" repeated old Caw, harshly. "A good deal, I should say. It means that on Sunday we could sit in a row by the side of the road from morning till night, and not a soul would think of harming us; but on a week day there would be a dozen guns pointed at us before we had been there five minutes. I want to give you a little advice before we begin our work. Don't caw so much. At the slightest provocation you set up such a noise that the whole neighborhood is down upon us, and as soon as they catch sight of us there will be an end to our fun. See if you can't remember this, and make up your minds to do your talking when you get home. Now for business.

"Do you see those little mounds over there beyond the potato patch? Well, that is for a late crop of corn, and every one of those mounds is full. You, Blackwing," continued old Caw, addressing the young crow who had asked the question a short time before, "remain on the top of this tree, and look all around you, particularly in the direction of the house and barn, and if you see any one coming, give one caw to warn us. And the rest of you, if you hear Blackwing caw, fly up at once, without a sound, taking care even not to flap your wings loudly, for if we succeed in escaping without being seen, we can return and finish our work."

Blackwing at once flew to the topmost branch of the tree, and the other members of the flock followed old Caw into the field of newly planted corn. Proceeding to one of the little mounds, the leader, with two or three skilful movements, scratched it open, and eagerly devoured the yellow kernels he found there. The others followed his example, and soon all were busy, and making sad havoc in the cornfield. They remembered the admonitions of old Caw, and preserved a discreet silence, stalking about among the little hills in their most dignified manner.

Suddenly a loud and continued cawing was heard from the sentinel on top of the tree, and up flew the marauders, cawing excitedly and flapping their long wings noisily, not stopping to look around until they had all lighted on various branches of the maple-trees, when they all talked and scolded together.

Old Caw flew to a tall tree whence all could see him. "Stop!" he called out, as soon as he could be heard amid the din of excited voices; "don't let me hear any more of this disgraceful proceeding. Stop this minute, I say!"

The discordant cawing gradually resolved into a confused murmur of voices, a few of the boldest still keeping up a low muttering of discontent; but so great was the excitement, that, as the last murmur died away, one persistent young crow (and we regret to have to acknowledge that it was one of old Caw's own grandsons) started a fresh complaint, and in a second the excitable creatures were all cawing together louder than ever.

Old Caw was almost beside himself. His weak, cracked voice was drowned in the general tumult, and driven to desperation at the insubordination of his followers, he rushed fiercely at them and distributed some sharp pecks indiscriminately. This had the desired effect, and at last order was restored.

"I am astonished at such outrageous behavior!" he said sternly, when he had regained his breath lost by this unusual exertion. "No, no more of it," he added quickly, as the persistent young crow who had once before started the commotion opened his beak to speak. " It is *my* business to settle this matter. In the first place, sir," he continued, turning to Blackwing, "why did you not caw *once*, as I ordered you, instead of raising such a hubbub? And, indeed, why did you caw at all? For I see no human being in sight, and I had especial information that the men of the family were away from home."

Blackwing's countenance fell under this severe reproof of his leader, but he hastened to defend himself.

" I kept watch as you directed," he began, " and saw nothing suspicious for awhile, until suddenly I beheld old Rough scurrying along as fast as he could come, and he stopped directly under the tree where I was watching. ' This is a pretty state of things,' he began, ' stealing my corn, you pack of thieves! Be off, or I 'll know the reason why!' I was naturally indignant, for I knew we had the best right to the cornfield, and I reminded him of it, whereupon he became vicious, and said the field belonged to him, and he did n't care what the owl had decided, and that he intended to trade with the corn. He became so abusive that I lost my temper, and forgot orders and called out to you."

"Where is the old miser now?" demanded old Caw, sternly.

"Oh, he slunk away as soon as I called out, and in all probability is hidden in some hole about here."

"I should like to see him," exclaimed old Caw, fiercely; "it would be some time before he meddled in my affairs again. His cornfield indeed! The old fellow carries things with too high a hand; and if I don't find a way to stop him, my name is n't old Caw."

One of the flock proposed to visit the cornfield again, and others fell in with the proposition; but old Caw silenced them by reminding them that it would be impossible now, at their greatest speed, to reach home before sunset, so much time had been spent in useless conversation.

"What harm would there be in remaining out a few minutes after dark?" asked one of the number.

"Have you forgotten Blinkeye?" asked old Caw, gravely; and at these words they silently came into line, and followed their discreet leader without any more discussion.

As soon as the flock of crows had left, a grizzled, shaggy object crawled out of a hole at the root of a tree, and the sharp and unpleasant features of old Rough appeared, an ugly grin displaying his long yellow teeth.

"You're very sharp, my friend Caw, I admit, but you are not so sharp as your humble servant. So you intend to stop me, do you, my fine fellow? Well, I'm ready for you. The first step toward it would be to stop the mouths of your followers, for thanks to their incessant jabbering I know all about their plans almost as soon as they do themselves. Now let me see what I'll do. As I am in the neighborhood, I'll take advantage of the opportunity to evict Bobtilla. Let's see, which is the shortest way?" And, sitting on his haunches, the old water-rat cast his shrewd eyes about him. His keen sight at once showed him the right direction, and he started off with great speed.

Before long old Rough stopped before a stone wall and looked about him. "It should be here," he said to himself. "I remember I took that large round stone as a landmark. Yes, here it is," and he at once went to a small hole that led under the wall.

The opening was too small for old Rough's large body, so in his sharp voice he called Bobtilla's name.

"Here I am," squeaked the little field-mouse, mildly; and in a moment she appeared before her dreaded landlord, and timidly asked the cause of his unexpected visit.

"I have come, madam," he replied, eying her sharply, "to give you notice to quit these premises."

"To quit these premises?" repeated Bobtilla, in astonishment.

"Yes, madam, I said to quit these premises," replied the old miser, harshly.

"Oh! what have I done that you should be so hard with me?" asked the little field-mouse, imploringly. "I have never done you or any one any harm."

"Have you kept your bargain, madam?" replied old Rough. "Where is the grain I expected to receive as rent for allowing you to remain on my premises?"

"I have been so unfortunate," pleaded the little mouse, in a tearful voice. "The winter was a hard one, and our stock of provisions was eaten up long ago. If you will only trust me a little while longer, the crops will then be ripe, and I will pay you double what I owe you!"

"Don't think to deceive me by your professions of poverty," said the miser, in so loud and harsh a tone that little Bobtilla started back terrified. "You think to make me believe you are poor, do you? Then please to inform me how those chestnut shells came to be lying there, will you?" And he pointed to some shells that were scattered on the ground.

"Oh! those were given me for my sick child," exclaimed Bobtilla, eagerly. "He has no appetite, and when you refused me the tender root I asked you for, some kind chipmunks who have recently moved here took pity on me and gave me a chestnut."

"So, you have been complaining of me to your neighbors, have you? Very well, madam, since they take such an interest in you, they are welcome to the benefit of your society. Let me see this place vacated by to-morrow at this time."

"Oh! have pity on me," said the poor little field-mouse, imploringly. "I can't move my sick child so soon. Do give me a little more time, at least."

"Not an hour!" replied the old miser. "To-morrow at this time I shall return, and if I find you still here," — he finished his sentence by a vicious snap of his long sharp teeth, that left Bobtilla in no uncertainty as to his intentions, and reduced her to a state of despair at the thought of the steps she should take to find a home for her little ones, and above all, for the sick one, whose condition gave her such anxiety.

As for old Rough, he went toward his home, happy in the thought of little Bobtilla's misery, and smiling to himself with great satisfaction, as he recalled her tremulous tones and tearful face, for never was old Rough so happy as when he had made others miserable.

Crossing the meadow, he went in the direction of the brook or ditch that led to his habitation, for he preferred the slimy and muddy borders of the ditch to any other path; and when he reached it, the sun had been down for some time, and twilight was gradually deepening.

The ditch was quite full from recent rains, and the soft mud felt cool and moist to his dry feet after his long journey; and so comfortable was he, that he proceeded very slowly, and recalled as he went the pleasures of the afternoon,— his success in preventing the crows from eating all the corn they wanted, and the misery to which he had reduced poor little Bobtilla. Before he knew it, darkness was upon him; but that he did not mind, for his keen eyes could see in the darkness as well as in the light.

So on went old Rough, with a light heart, when suddenly a loud hoot sounded just above him, and with a sudden start, he saw the bold Blinkeye, who could see clearly in the dim light, rushing fiercely toward him.

Large as the old water-rat was, Blinkeye was larger and stronger, and the old miser shuddered as he thought of those strong talons that had borne off so many prizes; and he remembered, too, how often he had laughed as he had seen the poor victims struggling in that relentless grasp.

Nearer and nearer came the huge owl, his glittering eyes fastened on his prey; and old Rough, his quick eyes taking in every point of the situation, in a few long leaps reached a place where the ditch widened, and with a vigorous bound plunged into the dark and muddy water, diving under the surface as his pursuer darted down to seize him.

The water-rat was old, and not so vigorous as in his youth; but his long life had taught him many useful lessons, and his experience more than compensated for the loss of his activity.

Now began a race for life, — the old rat diving and swimming and dodging about in the turpid water, every inch of which he was familiar with, and the large owl pursuing him, and often pouncing down, only to find his prey had escaped him; and now came an opportunity for the old water-rat to display one of those strategic movements for which he was remarkable, and which completely deceived even the wise owl.

The home of the water-rat was situated on a bank of the ditch where the water was deepest, and the owl felt sure that when the old miser left the water for his dwelling, which he would be sure to do, he could quickly seize him, and bear him away. The owl, however, did not know the precise spot of his victim's abode, and the wily rat passed it, and, turning unperceived in the deep water, swam back and entered his dwelling, while the discomfited owl was still hunting for him some distance down the stream.

"While in a melancholy voice, and with a strong French accent,
he sang the following lines."

CHAPTER V.

THE GREAT BASSO-PROFUNDO.

VERY great was Bobtilla's distress after
she had received the notice of evic-
tion from her hard-hearted landlord, and
all night she lay awake, trying to form

some plan for the future; but each one was abandoned almost as soon as it was formed, for the making of a new home is a matter for deep reflection, the happiness and welfare of a family depending so entirely upon it.

The spot where Bobtilla had hitherto resided, and which she was so cruelly compelled to leave, had many advantages of situation. It was so far removed from other dwellings that there was nothing to be feared from enemies, and as the little field-mouse was very particular about the society she chose for her children, she considered the seclusion a great advantage.

The longer Bobtilla pondered on the subject, the stronger became her conviction that her next move must be nearer the habitations of others, who would protect her in case old Rough should further persecute her. Having satisfied her mind on this point, she fell into a deep sleep, from which she did not awake until the day was well advanced. Then, perceiving the sun shining in through the small opening of her house, she started up hurriedly.

So deep had been the slumber of the little mouse, that during it all sense of the recollection of her trials had vanished, and for a moment she forgot the misery she had undergone before sleep came to her relief; but by degrees the feeling that all was not right stole over her, and gradually a full sense of her unfortunate situation returned.

Notwithstanding her natural timidity, Bobtilla was not entirely without energy, and she lost no time in useless repining; so hastily putting her house in order, and making her children comfortable, she set out with all speed to consult her new friends, the chipmunks.

The amiable couple heard with indignation how badly the field-mouse had been treated by the cruel miser, and they at once tried to think of a way to help her out of her difficulty.

"You had better come nearer to us," said Squirrello, when the little mouse had ended her sad story. "You will be farther away from old Rough, for he has not ventured into this neighborhood."

"Yes, and we can perhaps help you to a little food now and then," added Squirrella.

"You are very good to me," replied Bobtilla, gratefully. "I'm sure I don't know what I should do without you."

"Well, and why should n't we be? What are we here for, if it is not to help one another?" asked Squirrella.

"If everybody were of your mind, how easily we could live," sighed Bobtilla; "but as a general thing, the strong prey on the weak, and the rich on the poor."

"Well, at all events that is n't *our* way," replied Squirrella, cheerfully; "so now we

will decide on a new home for you. Let
me see, there is a nice place under that
large stone just behind you. I have often
thought it would be a good building-spot
for somebody. How does it strike you?"

"Capital!" exclaimed Bobtilla, joyfully.
The kind reception she had met with
raised her spirits wonderfully, for it meant
a peaceful home, where old Rough would
cease to persecute, and plenty of food for
her children until she could succeed in ac-
cumulating another stock of provisions.

So Bobtilla set to work with a will, and
soon had a convenient house made to her
satisfaction. When all was ready, she collected dried leaves and soft bits of moss,
and made a comfortable bed for her children, smiling with satisfaction as she contemplated the comfort she had succeeded
in effecting.

The praise of the two chipmunks, who
complimented her on her skill, was very

satisfactory, and she hastened to return to her children, in order to remove them to their new abode. Before the time set by old Rough, the little field-mice were safely established in their new quarters, and eating a good supper provided by their thoughtful friends the chipmunks.

While these events, of so much importance to Bobtilla and her family, were taking place, the two young crows were idling away their time, on the constant lookout for something with which to amuse themselves; and as they had not succeeded in appropriating the property of any one else or in doing any especial mischief, they felt that the day had not been a success, and time hung heavily on their hands. Alighting on a tree in the meadow, they cast their shrewd eyes about in all directions for any chance that might occur, and occasionally gave a languid caw.

Sitting thus idly, the tones of a deep

bass voice struck on their ears; and seated on the margin of the stream they beheld a large bull-frog gazing pensively into the water below, while in a melancholy voice, and with a strong French accent, he sang the following lines: —

> "Not always did I feel so bad,
> With eyes so heavy and heart so sad.
> Since many days I do not feel
> Desire to eat a hearty meal.
> No longer bugs and flies I eat,
> And grasshoppers with prickly feet.
> Indeed it was not always so;
> My feelings have received a blow.
> The melting voice of her I love
> Is now tuned for another cove.
> That fairy form, those eyes so yellow,
> Belong now to another fellow."

As the bull-frog ceased he sighed profoundly, and large tears rolled down his cheeks and splashed into the sluggish stream. The two young crows, rejoiced at the prospect of a diversion, flew down from the tree, and seated themselves on the bank of the stream opposite the mournful singer,

"What's up, Johnny?" they asked.

With a sigh that threatened to rend his capacious bosom, Johnny the basso replied, —

"She have deserted me. My sweetheart have left me for anozzer. I am in despair!"

"Who, the little green frog who lives down by the dam?"

"No!" replied the basso, indignantly; "it was no leetle green frog. My sweetheart is fine; she have one fine figure — Ah! qu'elle est charmante!"

"It was the little green one last week," answered the younger crow, dryly.

The mourner took no notice, but continued his lamehtations.

"She have left me for anozzer. She say, our voices they not blend well, — I, zee great basso-profundo! She prefer a tenor, she say. I 'ate a tenor, he squeal like one pig!"

"Who is he?" asked the elder crow.

"I know not how he call hisself, but I

will find him!" exclaimed the bull-frog, fiercely. "I will cr-crush zat tenor! He sall know what it is to insult zee greatest basso-profundo on zee earth. I will make zat tenor to tremble!"

"After you have found him," remarked the younger crow.

"But I will found him, I say!" exclaimed the excited basso. "I will hunt zee earth for zat tenor! My great talent, my vast wealth, they sall succeed in finding zat wr-r-etch who have deceived me, — *me*, zee greatest living basso-profundo on zee earth!"

"Why don't you consult old Blinkeye?" asked the elder crow.

"What you say he call hisself, — Blinkeye? I have nevare heard from him."

"Old Blinkeye is the wisest fellow about here, — knows all the laws of the woods by heart. Why, even my grandfather consults him, and my grandfather is no chicken, I can tell you."

"How know old Blinkeye anysing about my sweetheart? How will he find zis miser-rable tenor?"

"If he does n't know now, he will find out. He flies about all night, and learns a good many secrets that way. Oh, he 's a wise old fellow, is Blinkeye, and fierce too. Nobody knows how old he is."

"I sink he too old. Zee mind grow weak when old age come."

· "No, not a bit of it," replied the elder crow. "Then he is so strong and fierce, the tenor had better look out when he catches sight of him."

"I sink perhaps your fine Blinkeye eat me up. He say to hisself, 'Great basso-profundo fat and tender, — he make nice dinner. Tenor thin, — more bones as fat. I sink rather I eat great basso.'"

"He is only fierce at night. In the day-time he is as blind as a bat, and sits and thinks. Then, when night comes, he flies about, and it is better to keep out of his way.   Come, you'd better go and see him."

"Well, I go wiz you," answered the singer, after a moment's reflection.

Accordingly off set the three, the bull-frog hopping, and the crows walking behind him; but the bull-frog with his long leaps made much greater headway than the crows with their short steps, and the latter, when the frog was nearly out of sight, would use their wings to reach him, and at last adopted a gait between walking and flying.

The bull-frog was not in the habit of taking such long trips, and was obliged to halt occasionally; and these rests were spent in conversation, during which the basso recounted many valiant exploits he had achieved.

"Zis place is not large enough for so great a singer as I," said the bull-frog; "my talent is too great to rest in zis small place. One here has no taste; one knows not what

is musique.   When I lived in great meadow
far away, — ah! there it was fine! every
evening zey come, so many how zey could,
to hear zee great basso."

"Why did n't you stay there, Johnny?"
asked the younger crow.

"I was one fool," replied the bull-frog.
"I say, 'Zese peoples zey make me tired
wiz zere praise;' so I say to myself, 'My
friend, you sing too much, your fine voice
will ruin; better you move to some ozzer
place, where zere are not so many peoples.'
So I move here."

"And a very wise move it was," replied
the elder crow.   "But here we are, and
there sits old Blinkeye."

They stopped before the owl, who sat
silently on a tree, with his usual solemn
expression. He slightly turned his head
in the direction of his visitors, but it was
evident he did not see them.

"How do you find yourself to-day, Father

Blinkeye?" asked the elder crow. "We have brought a friend to consult you on a very important matter."

"Who is he, and what does he want?" demanded the owl.

The bull-frog hastened to introduce himself thus: "I am zee greatest basso-profundo on zee earth. Doubtless you have heard mention my great talent. I sing so deep,—zere is no basso who so deep sings. My *répertoire*, ah! it is *énorme*."

"What is your business with me?" inquired the owl, who remained unmoved by this announcement.

"My sweetheart she have left me," replied the bull-frog. "She have left me, *me*, zee great artist, for one tenor! I wish to find zat tenor! I wish to have revenge!" and he scowled fiercely at the recollection of his wrongs.

"What do you expect me to do about it?" asked Blinkeye, coldly.

"I sought zat perhaps you would have zee goodness to find zat tenor for me, sair."

"That is n't in my line," replied Blink-eye. "My business is to expound the laws of the woods."

"Zen will you be so kind, sair, as to tell me zee law zat will find zat tenor?" asked the basso, eagerly.

"Let me see where that comes in," said the owl, meditatively, and remained deep in thought, with one great yellow eye closed, and the other staring straight before him. This had such a solemn effect, that the basso felt sure such vast wisdom must procure for him the aid he desired.

"Aha!" exclaimed the owl, after awhile, and slowly unclosing his eye, "I have it. Now listen attentively, for I don't take the trouble of repeating these laws. Such a strain on my mind tires it and makes it dangerous for me.

> " ' Tirra, rirra, high and shrill
> Is heard throughout the meadow still ;
> And near the marshy bog is sung
> The musical, deep-toned a-hung!
> Take the one, and leave the other,
> And end this weary strife and bother.'

"Now leave me, that my mind may rest after such an effort," added the owl.

"But I know not what it mean, sair," exclaimed the basso, in bewilderment. "I know no more zan before, what I am to do. Will you have zee goodness to explain zat law to me."

"No," replied the owl, severely, "I will not. My business is to recite the law, and yours to understand it. If you don't, that's your loss. Now go."

"But, sair, — " began the basso. He did not have time to finish his sentence, however, for the two crows pushed and dragged him out of the owl's presence, promising to explain to him on the way home the meaning of the law of the woods recited by the owl.

"It's as plain as can be," said the elder crow, when they had succeeded in starting the basso toward home; "don't you see? 'Take the one and leave the other,' why, of course you'll take *the one*, and you'll leave the other when you only want *the one*, won't you?"

"But zat does not tell me where I sall find zee tenor," persisted the basso.

> "'Tirra, rirra, high and shrill,
> Is heard throughout the meadow still,' —

that's the tenor of course, with his high voice, and it tells you as plainly as possible that you'll find him in the meadow," explained the younger crow.

> "'And near the marshy bog is sung
> The musical, deep-toned a-hung,' —

that's *you* of course, with your deep bass. Now do you see your way clearly?"

This explanation appeared so very simple that the basso could but acknowledge it.

"Zee meadow is one large place," he said.

"Oh, well! now we know he is there, we'll find him for you, and the little brown frog will not be far off, you may be sure," said the elder crow.

Thus reassured, the bull-frog hopped briskly home, accompanied by the crows, who walked and flew by his side.

"I sank you, Messieurs, for your kindness," said the basso, when he stopped before his door, "and I sall know how to reward you. Au revoir, Messieurs," and, gracefully saluting his young friends, Johnny the basso hopped into his hole.

"The young crows' trick."

CHAPTER VI.

THE YOUNG CROWS' TRICK.

"WE shall have some fun with Johnny
the basso," said the younger crow,
as he stopped to gobble up several fat

crickets that had collected on a piece of
decaying fruit that lay by the roadside.

"An' is it that yees would be afther
taking the food from the mouths of a poor
widder an' her childer? Indade, an' it's
a long time since the poor craturs have
tasted the loike of these," said a voice
from behind; and suddenly turning, the
crows beheld a large fat toad, who watched
with indignation their lunch off the fat
crickets.

"Who are you, pray?" asked the elder
crow, "and why have n't we as much right
to eat these crickets as you?"

"It's the Widow O'Warty I am, wid
rispict to yees," replied the toad, with dig-
nity; "an' if it's the two foine wings of yees
meself possissed, it's not craping around
I'd be, to take the food from poor widders
an' childer."

"How did we know you wanted these
crickets?" asked the younger crow. "You

are welcome to them for all we care. We prefer our food well seasoned."

The Widow O'Warty became pacified under this partial concession, and resumed the plausible manner for which she was noted.

"It's me custom," she explained, "to sthroll out afther the light is quinched, in s'arch of a thrifle to ate. There do bees foine crickets about here, an' that's the troot av it."

The elder crow whispered to his brother, "Let's pass her off on Johnny as the brown frog he's lost."

"How can we, this great fat toad?" replied the other brother, in the same low tone.

"In the dark, you goose, he wouldn't know the difference, and we'd hide, and have lots of fun."

The younger crow cawed approval, the widow meanwhile eying them shrewdly, half suspecting that she herself was the subject of their whispered conversation.

"See here, Widow," began the elder crow, "you know Johnny the basso, don't you?"

"Is it the swate singer down by the bog ye mane?" asked the widow.

"Yes, I see you know him."

"It's the foine deep v'ice he possisses," replied the widow; "an' it's many a night meself has listened to the swate sounds."

"He's mashed on you, Widow," said the elder crow; "he's about as far gone as I ever saw any one."

"Be off wid yer nonsinse!" exclaimed the widow, not displeased at the news. "It's fooling yees are."

"Upon my honor, Widow," replied the elder crow, seriously; and addressing his brother he asked, "Did n't we hear him singing about her beautiful brown skin and her fine yellow eyes?"

"That we did," answered the younger crow, promptly; "and, my eyes! did n't he howl, though, when he talked about her?"

"I 'll not bel'ave yees," said the widow. "It 's making game of meself yees are."

"Not a bit of it, Widow," asserted the elder crow, earnestly. "True as we 're sitting here, we heard him singing about his sweetheart, who had a brown skin and yellow eyes."

"An' did he say 't was the Widow O'-Warty he was after m'aning?" asked the widow.

"He did n't exactly mention the name," replied the younger crow, evasively, "but he described you so correctly that he could n't have meant anybody else. We told him we 'd help him all we could."

"The Widow O' Warty is me name, an' me abode is opposite us; an' if he 's the gintilman I take him for, he will presint himself an' declare his intintions," said the widow, loftily.

"Then you 'll not be hard on him, will you, Widow?" asked the elder crow.

"Whin he has stated his intintions, it's meself that will consider his proposals," replied the widow, majestically.

"Then we 'll ease his mind by telling him you will allow him to call," replied the younger crow, as he and his brother flew off. When they were out of sight and hearing, they gave vent to the merriment they had been obliged to conceal from the watchful eyes of the widow, and their loud caws resounded through the wood.

Twilight was now approaching rapidly, and the two crows flew home as fast as their wings could carry them.

Early the next morning, the brother crows awoke, and were soon on their way to the dwelling of Johnny the basso. They found him sitting pensively on the border of the stream that flowed by his door, and abstractedly snapping at stray flies and bugs that came within reach of his long elastic tongue. Even ·these savory morsels were swallowed without any apparent enjoyment, but with a subdued and mournful countenance, as if he were performing some solemn rite.

"How are you this morning, Johnny?" called out his two visitors, as they seated themselves on a low bush that grew near by.

"I am miser-r-rable, my friends," replied the bull-frog, sadly, his large eyes swimming in tears. "I am not able to sleep. I sink on zee leetle brown frog. I weep, ah! how I weep for my sweetheart!"

"What should you say, Johnny, if we were to tell you we had found zee leetle brown frog?" asked the elder crow.

"What should I say?" exclaimed the bull-frog, with a sudden change of manner. "I should say zat it is incredible, messieurs, — zat it is impossible zat you should find zee leetle brown frog in so short a time."

"That's just what we have done, Johnny."

"Where is she?" exclaimed the singer, enthusiastically. "I fly to her, *mon ange, mon ange!*"

"Don't be in too great a hurry, Johnny," said the crow, cautiously. "You must n't take her by surprise. Wait till night comes, and then you can go and serenade her."

"It is impossible to wait until zee night come," replied the basso, excitedly; "now, zis minute, I fly to see zee leetle brown frog. But zee tenor? I forget zee miser-r-rable tenor who have stolen her from me. Where, I demand, is zis tenor?"

"We have n't found him yet," answered the elder crow, "but we will, in time.

He is probably not far off. You remember what the owl said,—

"'Tirra, rirra, high and shrill,
Is heard throughout the meadow still.'

He must still be in the meadow, you see."

"I go to fight wiz zat tenor!" exclaimed the bull-frog, furiously. "I will cr-r-rush zat tenor! But you have not say where is zee leetle brown frog."

"You see that small scrub-oak over in the field?" asked the elder crow, nodding his head in the direction of a small oak that grew by a stone wall. "Well, she lives in a hole in that wall. You will find her easily enough."

"I sank you, messieurs, for your kindness," said the basso, in his most gracious manner. "Permit me to make my adieu zat I may compose a song, zat zee leetle brown frog sall find zat my voice is so fine as before."

"Good-by," called out the crows, as they

flew away, " and good luck to you." They looked back as long as they were in sight, and saw that the basso sat motionless before his door, gazing silently into the depths of the stream.

The mischievous crows waited with impatience for the coming of night. It was not their habit to be out after sundown, but so eager were they to witness the result of their practical joke, that they resolved to pass the night in the neighborhood of the Widow O' Warty's abode, that they might see and hear what would happen. Accordingly, late in the afternoon they set out, and reached their destination soon after the sun had set.

A large maple-tree hung its branches over the wall near by, and on one of these branches the young crows perched, and sitting motionless, with their heads sunk between their shoulders, they awaited the development of their plan.

The eavesdroppers dared not converse, for fear of detection, and very hard it was for them to remain silent for so long a time, it being their habit to caw incessantly. Twilight soon appeared, and settled into darkness, and after what seemed to the listeners a long time, the moon rose over the tops of the forest trees, and gradually sailed into the sky.

This was a great relief to the young mischief-loving crows, for now they began to discern objects, and they felt sure that the beautiful moonlight would tempt the basso to steal forth to his trysting-place.

As the rays of the moon lighted up the wall under the tree on which the crows sat, they cautiously stretched forth their mischievous little black heads. At the door of her dwelling, in the shadow thrown by the scrub-oak, they discovered the matronly form of the Widow O'Warty, her prominent eyes shining in the moonlight.

Exchanging glances of suppressed merriment, the two crows, barely succeeding in smothering their laughter, again allowed their heads to sink between their shoulders, and resumed their former solemn attitude. They had not much longer to wait, for soon their shrewd eyes descried a dark form hopping through the grass, and rapidly approaching the scrub-oak.

When within a few feet of the widow's door, the new-comer stopped, and after a few ineffectual attempts to conquer his emotion, sang the following verses, in a voice that at first trembled perceptibly, but gradually increased in strength, until the full tones of his deep bass resounded through the still evening air.

> "The moon is on the bog,
>   The dew is on the lea;
>   The voice of every frog
>   Is calling, love, to me.
>   The noisy, gathering throng
>   Is calling on my name;
>   It clamors for a song
>   From singer of great fame.
>   A-hung!

"But the applause I hear
  Is nothing now to me;
I 'd give it all, my dear,
  For one sweet croak from thee.
All frogs, from far and wide,
  They linger 'round the bog,
They pine to be the bride
  Of the bull-basso-frog!
      A-hung!

"In dreams thy form I spy,
  And in my fond arms take;
But all those visions fly
  When in the morn I wake.
Then pray no longer hide,
  But let me hear thy voice;
Come to me, lovely bride,
  And bid my heart rejoice.
      A-hung!"

The full deep tones of the last "a-hung" had scarcely died away on the summer air, when the Widow O'Warty, who had, during the song, moved restlessly about, first on one foot and then on the other, suddenly gave vent to her emotions by hopping up to the singer and exclaiming in her shrill croak,—

"Faith, an' it 's meself that will put an ind to your suffering, me poor cratur!"

"Before the crows could reply, old Rough, who had listened with great satisfaction to the conversation, and had by degrees crept unperceived to the tree, hastened to reply."

CHAPTER VII.

DECLARATION OF WAR.

AT the Widow O'Warty's words, the melancholy singer gave a sudden start, and when the widow herself stood before him, he gazed in astonishment at her stout figure; but with native French courtesy he quickly recovered his self-possession, and bowed with great politeness to the smiling toad.

"An' is it so cruel ye take me to be as to kape ye longer waiting? 'Dade, an' I'll come till ye," said the widow, tenderly, and she hopped briskly to the bull-frog's side, and gazed smilingly into his face.

Johnny the basso was much disconcerted at the widow's advances, and for a moment he was silent. True, however, to his nature, in which was great courtesy toward the fair sex, he quickly suppressed the feeling of aversion that came over him, and answered politely,—

"Madame does me infinite *honneur*, but Madame mistakes; Madame doubtless has many suitors, and she does me the *honneur* to sink me one of them."

"Faith, an' it's not so fur out of the way ye are," replied the widow, slyly.

The basso found himself in an embarrassing situation. It was evident that this toad, whom he had never before seen, thought the words of his song addressed to her, and his sense of politeness made it difficult for him to tell her that she had made a mistake, and appropriated to herself sentiments that were intended for another.

"Is it that Madame does me zee *honneur* to sink zat zee words of my song were addressed to her?" asked the basso.

"Fwhat ilse, in the name of the howly saints, would ye have me think, whin it's afore me door ye sthand? *Av coorse* I considered the worrds addrissed to meself."

"If it had been my good fortune to have met Madame, I could not have found words ardent enough to express zee grand passion wiz which Madame would have inspired me," answered the basso, with great politeness.

"Thin why in the worrld did ye station yeself afore me door, if the worrds were addrissed to another party?" asked the widow, angrily.

"It is because one told me that here lived her whom I sought, — whom I sall always seek while I have life," answered the bull-frog, with intense feeling.

"Fwhat is the name av the raskill that tould ye this was not me abode?" asked the widow, indignantly.

"Two young crows have informed me," replied the bull-frog, "and zey sall give me satisfaction. Zey sall learn what it is to trifle wiz zee great basso."

"An' it's the same as tould me ye had lost your heart to meself, an' apprised me of your coming the night," answered the widow.

"I will seek zem in zee morning," said the basso, fiercely. "Zey sall answer to me for their impertinence. *Au revoir*, Madame.

Believe me, I sall lose no time to avenge zis insult;" and as he hopped away, the two young crows, no longer able to conceal their merriment at the success of their joke, flew away, laughing "Caw, caw, caw."

This naturally added to the basso's vexation; but the young crows were soon far away, their "caw, caw, caw" being audible as long as they were in sight.

It was at an early hour the next morning that the indignant basso set off to find these mischievous young crows who had caused him so much annoyance; and, early as it was when he reached their home, he found only old Caw, who was perched on his favorite tree in a meditative attitude, and the mother of the young crows, who was engaged in feeding her young family, scolding and complaining all the while.

So engrossed was the mother-crow, that it was some time before the bull-frog succeeded in attracting her attention. As for old Caw, it was impossible to tell whether he was aware of what went on about him, for his one eye was apparently closed, and he seemed in that indifferent state of mind that extreme old age produces. Those who knew him well, however, knew that this was a trick of his to escape observation, and that he was never more alert than when he was apparently in this apathetic state.

"What do you want?" asked the crow-mother, when the bull-frog had succeeded in attracting her attention.

"Zere are two very mischievous young crows whom I seek, Madame," answered the basso. "I wish to speak wiz zose young crows."

"There are not any of that description here," replied the crow-mother, shortly.

"Pardon me, Madame, but one has told me zat I sall find zem here, — zat zey are your sons."

" They told you wrong, then, for my sons are steady, hard-working fellows, who never did any mischief in their lives."

The old crow from his tree here gave an abrupt croak, which to the bull-frog sounded like an expression of surprise; but when the bull-frog quickly glanced at him, he found him with such a sleepy and imbecile expression on his pinched countenance that he concluded he must have been mistaken.

" It cannot be that I have wrong," said the bull-frog, firmly. " Zee mischievous young crows of whom I speak live here. I have seen them often. It was yesterday zat zese young crows played me a sad trick, — I wish to speak wiz zem."

" If it were yesterday, it could n't have been my sons, for they were at home all day," answered the crow-mother, decidedly.

The bull-frog, happening to glance in the direction of old Caw, caught sight of his one eye wide open, and the bull-frog imagined that he detected a particularly amused look in that expressive feature ; but the eye closed again so sleepily and naturally that he concluded he must have been again mistaken.

The bull-frog was far from being convinced that the mother-crow was telling the truth about her sons, but courtesy prevented him from pushing the matter further.

"If Madame their mother says her sons to have been at home yesterday, zen I have nozzing to say," said the bull-frog, courteously. "I have zee *honneur* to wish Madame good-day ;" and the discomfited singer ended the unsatisfactory interview.

As the bull-frog hopped toward home, he revolved in his mind the best course to take in order to bring about a meeting with the young crows, for he felt sure their mother would put them on their guard against him ; when suddenly he was surprised in his meditations by a caw over-head, and looking quickly up, he beheld the old crow Caw sitting on a branch above him.

Old Caw was wide awake now, and his one eye beamed with as much vivacity and intelligence as that of any young crow could have been capable.

"Stop a minute, friend Johnny," said the old crow; "don't be in such a hurry."

The bull-frog, thus addressed, stopped, breathing fast from his exertions, and regarded the self-possessed old crow with an angry countenance.

"Don't be in such a hurry; take it easy, Johnny," said the old crow, coolly.

"You have zee advantage of me, sair," said the bull-frog, haughtily; "you appear to be familiar wiz my name. I have not zee great *honneur* to be acquainted wiz zee illustrious name of Monsieur."

"Oh, yes, I know you well, Johnny,—

I 've heard you croak often enough on moonlight nights," replied the crow, with exasperating coolness, at the same time bringing his one eye to bear on the indignant bull-frog.

"You insult me, sair," exclaimed the basso, excitedly. "It is that you have no soul for musique. Croak, you say! You say zee greatest living basso on zee earth croak!"

"Don't get excited, Johnny, I did n't intend any insult," said the old crow, persuasively. "I came after you to be of service."

But the insult still rankled in the singer's capacious bosom, and his great throat swelled and vibrated with wounded pride, as he repeatedly gave expression to his indignation.

"Oh, come, Johnny, cool down and hear what I 've got to tell you," said old Caw, soothingly. "You want to find the young crows who played a trick on you, don't you?"

The bull-frog made a great effort to recover his self-possession, and with much difficulty swallowed his resentment.

"Yes," he answered, after a great inward struggle, "I wish to know where to find zose young crows."

"The old lady fibbed, of course," said old Caw. "They *are* her sons, and I knew they were up to some mischief, for they went away yesterday afternoon, after whispering and giggling together, and did n't come home until this morning."

"Can you tell me where I sall find zem?" asked the basso, eagerly.

"Yes, I can," replied the old crow. "I listened when they thought I was asleep, and overheard their plans. They intend to hang around old Rough's place until he has gone out on one of his foraging expeditions; and when he is out of the way, they have planned to steal into his hole and help themselves to a fine bit of pork-rind they saw him scurrying off with yesterday. You'll find them somewhere in that neighborhood."

"I sank you, sair," said the bull-frog, politely, "for your very kind information. I sall go at once to Monsieur Rough's abode. Adieu, Monsieur Corbeau;" and with his usual impetuosity, the bull-frog hurried away in the direction of the old miser's dwelling.

Old Caw followed the bull-frog with his one eye as long as he was in sight, and then gave expression to a caw of satisfaction. "I think this will make me even with you for stealing my pig's ear, you young thieves," said the old crow to himself. "I made you think I hid it purposely, to teach you shrewdness in discovering hidden treasures, but it was n't true. Old, Caw must be getting old indeed, when two young fools get the better of him. Yes, I think this last move of mine will make us even;" and having uttered these sentiments, old Caw slowly wended his way homeward.

Meanwhile, the bull-frog, his heart set on confronting the crows with their treachery, proceeded as fast as his slow powers of locomotion enabled him to travel. At last, after a tedious journey, he reached the neighborhood of old Rough, and halting within a short distance of the miser's abode, glanced about him.

There was the old water-rat's dwelling just above the ditch, and at a short distance behind it grew a fine tree, among whose branches the frog detected two black motionless objects.

"Zee old crow had right," said the singer, to himself, "zere are zee two mischievous crows."

Stopping long enough to recover his

breath, and keeping his eyes on the two black objects in the tree, the bull-frog proceeded toward the tree, followed at a distance by a dark object that slid through the tall meadow grass, that halted as he halted, and that proceeded as he proceeded.

This dark object that followed the bull-frog, and was so careful to escape detection, was old Rough, the water-rat.

The bull-frog proceeded boldly to the foot of the tree and stopped, and the water-rat concealed himself behind a large stone not far off, and within convenient hearing distance. No other living creatures were in sight, except a swallow that flew noiselessly over the meadow, occasionally swooping on some unfortunate insect, and then soaring swiftly high into the air.

"Is it zat you are zere, my fine Messieurs!" cried the bull-frog, fiercely, looking up at the young crows perched far above him.

"Yes, friend Johnny, it is that we are here. How's the little brown frog you serenaded last night?"

"It is zat I wish to confront you wiz your treachery, Messieurs," exclaimed the bull-frog, furious at this taunt. "I wish to tell you zat you are great imposters; zat you have deceived Madame La Warty; zat you have deceived me, — me, zee great singer, I say! But I have my great reputation to avenge! I have Madame La Warty's *honneur* to defend."

"Oh, bother! the widow does n't mind that," said the younger crow. "You don't mean to say she is n't the brown frog you were looking for?"

"Madame La Warty is one great fat toad, Monsieur!" exclaimed the bull-frog, indignantly. "Did you sink zat I, zee great singer, would have one toad for his sweetheart! No, sair, zat is not possible! Zee young, zee beautiful are for zee great basso-profundo."

"How did you expect us to know the difference?" asked the elder crow. "They look alike to us, any way."

The singer glared fiercely on the impudent young crow. "I sall have revenge," he cried in his deepest tones; "you sall answer to me for zis insult. *Mon Dieu!* he say a fat toad look like a frog!"

"Well, we did n't know," said the younger crow. "We were told she was the one, and we thought we were doing you a favor to tell you. How could we tell you 'd make such a row about it?"

"Who is it zat told you Madame La Warty was zee leetle brown frog?" inquired the singer, fiercely.

Before the crows could reply, old Rough, who had listened with great satisfaction to the conversation, and had by degrees crept unperceived to the tree, hastened to reply, —

"Why don't you tell the whole story,

boys? Why not say that it was Bobtilla who told you? If any one is to blame it is she. You only repeated her words, you know."

"Yes, it was Bobtilla who told us," asserted the young crows, boldly, greatly surprised at the information, but glad to throw the blame upon anybody's shoulders.

"Who is Bobtilla? I have not zee pleasure of her acquaintance," said the bull-frog, addressing the water-rat.

"A meddlesome field-mouse," explained the miser, viciously. "She looks meek enough, but she is a mischievous creature, and takes delight in getting honest people, like our young friends here, into trouble."

"I cannot demand satisfaction of a lady," exclaimed the bull-frog; "but I will challenge zee whole race of field-mice. I will exterminate zee race. Zey sall know what it is to insult zee great singer. It sall be war, until every field-mouse sall die."

"Now, Bobtilla," said old Rough to himself, as he went toward his home, "we will see how much help your new friends can give you. It will not pay, my dear madam, to stand out against old Rough; he's more than a match for you, my dear! War against the field-mice, friend Johnny! Just what I want. I could n't have arranged matters better myself. Now their houses will be destroyed, and what a harvest for me!" And the old miser squeaked with joy, as he slipped through the meadow grass, and his long nose moved viciously about, as it always did when he experienced any strong emotion.

"There is no need to tell me, kind friends, said a trembling little voice; and Bobtilla stood before them."

CHAPTER VIII.

SWIFT PUTS BOBTILLA AND THE SQUIRRELS ON THEIR GUARD.

OLD Rough was not the only listener to the conversation between the bull-frog and the two young crows. The chimney-swallow Swift, who at the time was sailing over the meadow, apparently intent only on securing the finest insects, had heard every word that was said.

No sooner had the conversation ceased and the party separated, than the swallow with a few strong strokes of his long wings soared high above the meadow, until he looked like a little black speck. Soon, however, the black speck seemed to remain stationary, and then it grew larger and larger, as it rapidly descended, and alighting on the wall where the chipmunks dwelt, sat pluming its glossy feathers in a very skilful manner.

So engrossed was the swallow in his occupation that he appeared to be unconscious of everything that went on about him. Even the loud cawing of the two young crows, who alighted on a neighboring tree, did not take his attention from his task, and he was evidently unaware of the presence of the little chipmunk Squirrello, who first peeped timidly out of his hole, and after a careful survey of the country, grew bolder, and seated himself on top of the wall.

Little Bobtilla, too, from her house under the large stone, peeped out with her bright eyes, thinking it more prudent to remain in her doorway; the swallow, however, did not notice her any more than he did the squirrel, and continued to sit on the tree, picking apart his thick feathers. Before long the young crows flew away, and no sooner were they fairly out of sight than the swallow abruptly finished his toilet, and flew upon the top of the wall in front of Squirrello.

"I recognized you at once, Swift," said Squirrello; "but I thought by your manner that you did n't wish to have me notice you, so I kept still."

"And quite right you were," replied Swift. "The truth is that I have news of importance, and did n't want those mischie-vous crows to hear it."

Squirrello came nearer to the swallow, and awaited with anxiety the news he had to tell. Little Bobtilla, from her doorway under the large stone, inclined one ear toward the swallow, and listened with breathless interest.

"Just now," began Swift, "I observed those two young crows who have just gone sitting very still on a tree that grows just behind old Rough's den. They are always so noisy and restless that I knew their unusual silence meant mischief, so I re-solved to keep about and find out what it meant. They had n't the least suspicion that I was watching them, for I took care to keep at a safe distance.

" Before long I saw Johnny the basso hopping along, and he stopped under that very tree. Old Rough crept slyly after him, and hid where he could overhear every

word that was said. As soon as Johnny
found sufficient breath to speak, he re-
proached the crows for having played a
trick on him. I lost some of the conversation, not daring to venture too near;
but I gathered that the crows had tried to
pass the Widow O'Warty off for some one
else. Before long old Rough came forward,
and threw the whole blame on little Bobtilla, and the crows acknowledged that it
was she who had given them their information. Whereupon Johnny, who prides
himself on his gallantry to the fair sex,
said that since a lady was to blame, he
could n't call her to account, but that he
would make the whole race of field-mice
responsible, and declared war upon the spot.
This seemed to please old Rough greatly,
for he went off chuckling and muttering to
himself."

Poor little Bobtilla's state of mind, as
she heard these words, can be better ima-

gined than described. She had, since her removal to the neighborhood of the chipmunks, begun to know what peace of mind was; and now all at once her hopes were shattered, and she felt that in no place would she be secure from the wrath of old Rough, which pursued her, go where she would. Shaking with fear, she remained in her doorway, too agitated to move or speak.

"What an outrage!" exclaimed Squirrello, as the swallow finished his recital. "Why, Bobtilla is the meekest and most amiable of creatures, — she wouldn't harm a fly, — and I know she never spoke a word to either of those mischievous crows. It is a trick of old Rough, to spite poor little Bobtilla."

"What is a trick of old Rough; and what has Bobtilla, of all creatures, to do with it?" asked Squirrella, who had heard her husband's indignant tones, and now appeared on the wall beside him, to learn the cause of the excitement.

The story was told over again to Squirrella, and her indignation was even greater than her husband's.

"I never heard anything so mean in all my life!" exclaimed the kind-hearted Squirrella. "I should think that poor little creature had suffered enough at old Rough's hands, without this new persecution. However, I don't see what old Rough will gain from a war between the mice and frogs; he will not fight himself."

"He evidently considers it for his advantage," answered the swallow, "for he went off in fine spirits. If the frogs are victorious, they will certainly destroy every mousehole in the meadow and woods; and it's my private opinion that old Rough will slink around during the battle, and steal everything he can lay his paws on."

"Fortunately we are out of the way," said Squirrello.

"I'm not so sure about that," replied Swift. "I would n't risk it. If I were you, I'd be on the safe side, and move farther into the woods, and make your home more secure. Bobtilla, too, must move, for old Rough would be sure to visit her house first of all."

"Dear me!" sighed Squirrella, "here we are, so comfortably settled for life I thought, and now we must move again. I don't see how I can have the patience to go through it all again. I have heard that three moves are equal to a fire; I should say that two were equal to an earthquake."

"I don't very well see what else can be done, my dear," replied her husband. "You are the last one, such an anxious mother as you are, to feel secure while war is raging around you."

"Yes, I suppose there is nothing else to be done," sighed Squirrella.

"After we have moved, and are settled

in our new home, I am sure you will think yourself much better off, and wish you had chosen the place before," said Squirrello, who always looked on the bright side of affairs.

"I forgot all about Bobtilla," exclaimed Squirrella. "Poor thing, she thought herself so safe here, — how can I tell her the bad news?"

"There is no need to tell me, kind friends," said a trembling little voice; and Bobtilla stood before them. "I have heard all, and also your kind plans for my safety, and I can truly say that I do not feel so badly about myself as I do to think that out of your kindness to me, you must have the trouble of moving again."

"Nonsense!" answered Squirrella, briskly; "what have you to do with it? Do you suppose I want to live on the battle-field, as you may say? No, indeed; I prefer to move away where I shall not have fighting going on before my eyes."

"I know very well," persisted Bobtilla, " that I am the cause of all this trouble, for old Rough will not let me rest as long as I have a home to live in; and he will persecute all those who are kind to me. I know him so well that I feel sure he has done me this ill turn because I have found new and influential friends to protect me."

" Well, after all, it does n't matter," replied Squirrella, cheerfully. " The woods are quieter, and the air is purer there, and I am sure we shall be better off. So let's decide on a spot; and the sooner we start about it the better."

"I have a place in my mind," said the swallow, " and if one of you will come with me, you can see what you think about it."

Squirrello decided to accompany the swallow, and both set off, — the squirrel running along the highest boughs and jumping lightly from one tree to another, while little Swift soared high above him, often flying far out of sight, but always returning to point out the way.

At last the swallow stopped before a stately old oak-tree, whose sturdy branches were nearly bare of leaves, but whose topmost boughs were still clad with green leaves, as reminders that some vitality yet remained to the aged tree. The sturdy roots, that had resisted many a tempest, protruded above the soft turf, and seemed so formed purposely, that they might serve as homes for little animals in search of a dwelling-place.

" There," said the swallow, pointing out the spot, " there is a house already built for you; and all you have to do is to make it soft and comfortable for your family."

Nothing could be more desirable for a dwelling, and Squirrello returned to his little wife, and related to her what he had found. Both together visited the new home, and Squirrella was, if possible, even more pleased with the place than her husband had been, her motherly instincts at once divining that no place in the whole world could be so well suited for a young family like hers. The protecting roots of the old tree made it safe against the depredations of enemies, and the long, strong branches were just right for her children to run about on,—so much better and safer for them than running along the stone wall in sight of the whole world. Also under the roots of the old tree was a hole that looked as if it were made expressly for Bobtilla and her young family.

Thus the happy couple discussed their plans, and at once busied themselves in collecting soft, dry moss, and carrying it into their new house. Squirrella was so delighted with the appearance of the bed her children were to have, that she lay down in it, to see if it were as comfortable as it looked; and she declared that it surpassed her most sanguine expectations, and that it was utterly impossible for any bed in the universe to be as comfortable as her children's was.

Then Bobtilla was brought to see the place, and the timid little creature was greatly pleased with it, and felt that in that peaceful wilderness she might be freed from the persecutions of old Rough. Poor little Bobtilla! she was fast experiencing that the strong prey on the weak in the struggle for life!

The little field-mouse, also, went to work, like the conscientious mouse she was, and dug out her house as far as she could under the roots of the old tree, and then made it soft and warm for her family. When this was done, at the suggestion of her friends the squirrels she skilfully concealed the entrance with moss, leaving only an opening large enough to squeeze her little body through.

The squirrels viewed Bobtilla's work with great satisfaction, and concluded that even old Rough, shrewd as he was, could never detect it as the abode of a family; and, indeed, all three agreed in thinking that no living creatures had ever been so fortunate in securing such choice locations and in making such comfortable homes.

Then the squirrel family and the mouse family were removed to their new quarters, and all was peace and contentment once more.

While these new homes were being prepared, the news of the impending war was spreading rapidly over the adjoining meadows and fields, and soon all knew the fact that the frogs had declared war against the field-mice. Everywhere, in the meadows and fields, groups of field-mice were collected, discussing the exciting news; and every evening on the borders of the ditch, and on the edges of the bog, frogs of all sizes and ages were heard croaking over the same topic.

Among all the animals, old Rough the water-rat was the one who seemed to derive the most satisfaction from the prospect of war. He fairly gloated over the thought that the dwellings of the field-mice would be destroyed, and he should reap the benefit of the stock of provisions that the industrious little creatures had collected with so much pains.

More agreeable even than this was the thought that when the war was ended, and their homes and property destroyed, the field-mice would come to him to trade for provisions, and then he could make his own terms.

Dwelling on these pleasant themes, old Rough remembered Bobtilla, and he felt happier still as he reflected on the misery in store for her. So pleasant was it to imagine what her sufferings would be, that he resolved to make her a call, and witness her despair as he recounted to her the misery in store for her. Thus elated by this generous resolve, the old miser set briskly off for Bobtilla's abode, and in due time found himself before her door. Not hearing any signs of life, he called aloud,—

"Bobtilla!"

Not a sound was heard in response, and old Rough wondered at this, for the tones of his harsh voice had never before failed to bring the little field-mouse trembling before him. Once more he called, and more loudly; but all was silent, and he walked up to the house and looked in.

All was so still inside that the old miser was convinced that the house was empty, and he fell into a great rage as he realized that his victim had escaped. In his ungovernable passion he tore away the earth from before the entrance to the former dwelling of the field-mouse, and his strong paws soon disclosed the vacated home. Not a vestige of Bobtilla's family remained, save the bed of leaves and moss where they had so lately reposed.

"Won't I make you speak though, my lady!" exclaimed the old water-rat, savagely.

"You must find her first, my friend," said a voice from above the wall.

"So intent were they on their sport, that they did not perceive two young crows who perched on the very tree at whose roots they lived."

CHAPTER IX.

THE CROWS PLAN A SURPRISE FOR OLD ROUGH.

OLD Rough glanced fiercely in the direction of the speaker's voice, and beheld, seated unconcernedly on a tree, the chimney-swallow, Swift.

"I intend to find her, sir," answered old Rough, viciously, his nose moving about rapidly in his excitement. "I can assure you it is not so easy to escape me as you imagine."

"How much will you bet that you find Bobtilla within a week?" asked the swallow.

"I will find her within three days," replied old Rough, savagely; "and let me tell you that her friends who interest themselves in her welfare had better look out!" and old Rough went toward the dwelling lately inhabited by the little chipmunks. In vain the old water-rat peeped into the hole, and glanced sharply around him, — not a trace of the chipmunk family was to be found.

"You'll have to leave your card; they're evidently not at home," said the swallow, coolly, as the old water-rat looked about him wrathfully.

"I'll thank you to mind your own business, sir," responded old Rough. "If I thought you were at the bottom of all this, I'd—" he stopped, with a vicious snap of his teeth.

"You'd what?" asked the swallow, calmly.

"I'd take care that you never repeated the trick," said old Rough. "Now that I think of it, I believe you are the swallow that was flying about pretending to catch insects, when my friends and I were talking together. Eavesdropper!"

"Yes, I am the very one, just as you are the water-rat that was squatting down behind the big stone, you know, to over-hear what the crows and Johnny the basso were talking about."

"And you gave warning to Bobtilla, and advised her to move!" said old Rough, ignoring entirely the allusion to his own eavesdropping.

"Just so," replied the swallow, calmly; "I not only advised Bobtilla and the squirrels to move, but I selected a spot for them where you'll never find them if you hunt till you're blind."

"I shall find them before three days have passed," asserted the water-rat. "I have influence sufficient to discover them if they are on the face of the earth, and I can assure you that my revenge will be all the sweeter for having to wait."

"Yes, if time adds to the pleasure of revenge, yours will have a chance to grow considerably."

"And I shall not forget the little favor you have done me in trying to frustrate my plans," snarled the old rat.

"Don't mention it; you are quite welcome," responded the swallow, with great good-humor, as he rose into the air and soared out of sight.

Old Rough remained quite still for

awhile, thinking over the best course to pursue to recover Bobtilla, and he concluded he could not do it without some help. To whom should he apply? Old Blinkeye was the first who came to his mind as the most likely to find them out; but he was out of the question, for if the fierce owl discovered Bobtilla and the squirrels, he would most surely keep them for himself, such tender morsels as they would make.

Next the two young crows came into the water-rat's mind; but how could he trust such unreliable fellows? To be sure, it would take cleverer young fellows than they to dupe the wary old water-rat, but still he did n't dare trust them.

How about old Caw? Old as he was, his one eye could see farther than any other pair, and the old thief would do anything that paid well. The longer the miser considered the matter, the more convinced he became that old Caw was the one to do the business for him.

All the while the water-rat had been forming this plan, if little Bobtilla or the squirrels had seen him, they might well have trembled for their safety, for a most unpleasant spectacle he presented, as he sat on his haunches, his small sharp eyes gleaming with malice, and his long nose moving incessantly.

Having come to the conclusion that old Caw was the one to help him out of his difficulty, the old water-rat lost no time in seeking him. The old crow was at home; indeed he seldom ventured away from it, except in search of food, and then he usually made solitary expeditions into the woods, where he detected appetizing morsels that the younger crows had not discovered. Favorite haunts he frequented, where he unearthed the delicate tidbits he had secreted, and many a sumptuous repast he made on some particularly dainty bit his young grandsons had buried for their own especial food.

To-day, however, the old crow was at home, and sitting on his favorite perch, his one eye closed, and his head sunk between his high shoulders. He was apparently unaware of the water-rat's approach, and old Rough contemplated him for awhile in silence.

"The old thief is as wide awake as I am," said old Rough to himself, as he watched the slumbering crow. "He is looking at me out of one corner of his sharp old eye, and pretends to be asleep.—Hallo, friend Caw!" he called out, when he had grown tired of waiting.

The old crow languidly opened his one eye half way, and glanced about in a direction opposite from where the water-rat was stationed; then he drowsily closed it again, and continued his nap.

"Hallo, old Caw, I say!" called out the water-rat again, somewhat louder.

"What say?" slowly demanded old Caw, again opening his eye, and inclining one ear toward his visitor.

"Something new for the old fellow to be deaf," muttered the old miser to himself. "Hallo! I said," he shouted, as the old crow showed symptoms of relapsing into another nap. "Can't you keep awake long enough to hear what I have to say? I'll make it for your interest."

At these words, the old crow's drowsiness and deafness disappeared together, and he assumed an attentive attitude, while the old water-rat began his story.

"I came to ask you to discover the hiding-places of a certain field-mouse, one Bobtilla by name, and a pair of chipmunks who have gone off with her. If you'll find out where they are, I'll pay you well for it."

" What 'll you give ?" asked the old crow, shrewdly, with his head on one side, and his half-closed eye on the rat.

" I 'll put you in the way of getting a fine sheep's pluck," replied old Rough.

" Yes, I know farmer Smith has just killed a sheep," answered old Caw, quietly.

" But you don't know where the best part of the pluck is, the tender liver, that melts in your mouth," added the water-rat.

The old crow in answer gave a short caw expressive of indifference, and then began to show symptoms of a return to the drowsy condition in which the old rat had found him.

" Will you trade, or not ?" asked old Rough.

" That depends upon how much you 're willing to give. I can't say I 'm hankering after the job," answered old Caw.

" I 've just told you what I 'll give," said old Rough, impatiently, — " a rich sheep's liver, that when it's been buried a couple of weeks will fairly make your mouth water."

"Not half enough," replied Caw, calmly. "On the whole, I don't think I care to undertake the job."

"What job?" called out a voice; "if it's a paying one, I'm your crow," and the two young crows alighted on the tree beside their grandfather.

Having failed with the old crow, the water-rat found there was nothing to be done but to avail himself of the assistance of the younger crows; and after much haggling on both sides, the young crows decided to undertake the job, provided the old miser would give them the sheep's liver and a fine piece of pork-rind which they knew him to possess. Having thus concluded the bargain, the old water-rat departed, well-satisfied with his morning's work, and confident that he would shortly have Bobtilla and the chipmunks in his power.

When he was well out of sight and hearing, old Caw addressed his grandsons thus, —

"What induced you to undertake this thing?"

"Why, the sheep's liver and pork-rind, of course," they replied.

"When do you expect to get possession of them?" asked old Caw.

"When we've found out where the field-mouse and squirrels are, of course," replied his elder grandson.

"There's no *of course* about it," quietly answered old Caw. "Don't you know the miser never pays his debts?"

The young crows looked rather sheepish at this, but assured their grandfather that they would find a way to be even with the old miser if he didn't pay up.

"I advise you to be cautious how you

play any tricks on the old fellow," said old Caw, "for he's sharper than you are. Don't you suppose *I*'d have undertaken the job if I had thought it would pay?"

"What would you advise us to do about it?" asked the younger grandson.

"Well, since it's in the family, I don't mind giving you some advice," replied the old crow. "Pretend you have found the places he wants, and then when he has gone there, go and help yourselves to the sheep's liver and pork-rind. That's the surest way I know of."

Having imparted this valuable information, old Caw was soon asleep in earnest, and his two grandsons sat whispering over their plans. Whatever conclusion they arrived at was evidently very satisfactory, for they chuckled gleefully over it.

All this time, the objects of this wicked plotting were safe in their new homes, enjoying the pure air of the forest, and sporting among the trees and over the soft turf, never dreaming but that this state of security would last forever. Occasionally a bird passed over the tree at whose foot they were hidden, or stopped to rest on one of its branches, but no one offered to molest them.

One day, Bobtilla was out in search of food for her family, and the squirrels were absent on the same errand. Their young families were left at home by themselves, with instructions not to leave their homes.

The day was fine, and all was so quiet in the woods that it was hard for these active young creatures to remain cramped in their small quarters. One of Bobtilla's children ventured timidly to the door, and peeped cautiously out. At the same moment he appeared at the opening, his bright little eyes fell on one of the squirrel's children, who was likewise tempted to obtain a breath of fresh air.

After a short conversation, they were joined by their brothers and sisters. A consultation ensued, in which they agreed that it was positively injurious to the health of all to remain longer in such close quarters, and that a little exercise in the pure air would be to their advantage, and the very thing their parents would desire for them under the circumstances.

Having arrived at this wise conclusion, the little field-mice and their squirrel neighbors ventured out of their dark homes, and were soon frisking about in the liveliest manner, — the squirrels racing over the trees and stumps, and the little mice running about below. So intent were they on their sport, that they did not perceive two young crows, who perched on the very tree at whose roots they lived.

"Hallo!" called out the crows, and at the sudden sound they all scampered into their holes.

"Perhaps we can find out something from them," said the crows to each other; and they remained silently on the tree.

Before long one of the young squirrels, more venturesome than the rest, became emboldened to peep out of his house, and beheld the two young crows quietly seated on the tree.

"What's the trouble, sonny?" asked one of the crows; "we will not hurt you. Come out, and finish your game."

A whispered conversation followed inside the squirrel house, and at last they all ventured out again, and sat in a row on their little haunches, looking up curiously at their black visitors.

"We are alone, and our mother told us to stay in the house," remarked the squirrel who had first ventured out.

"You mind well," said the elder crow; "shows you've been well brought up."

"You see we have not been out since

we moved," continued the squirrel, who became communicative as soon as he found the new-comers were kindly disposed; "and we were tired of staying in that dark hole. It 's awfully hard to be so cramped up, you know."

"I should think so," replied the crow. "Why don't your friends come out again?" Then he added in a low tone to his brother, "He says they have moved,— you may be sure it 's the ones we 're looking for."

"They are very timid," replied the squirrel; "and Bobtilla told them if they went out, old Rough would be sure to catch them."

"So they are Bobtilla's children, are they?"

"Yes," replied the squirrel.

"Well, go on with your play," said the crows, and away they flew, having gained all the information they wanted, without the slightest effort on their part.

"Now for old Rough. We 'll find him

and direct him to the right spot. Won't he be surprised, though?" said the younger crow; and the thought of what they were about to do afforded them such delight that their loud laughter caused them to fly in a very disorderly manner, bumping against each other, and conducting themselves very riotously.

"The numerous barns and sheds, well stocked with horses and cattle, gave evidence of the prosperity of the owner."

CHAPTER X.

OLD ROUGH IN DANGER.

THE next day, the two young crows started out at an early hour, and continued their flight until they approached a large farm, situated far back from the road. The numerous barns and sheds, well stocked with horses and cattle, gave evidence of the prosperity of the owner. Casting their sharp eyes about, the two crows selected a large chestnut-tree that grew in the rear of the buildings, whose dense foliage promised a safe hiding-place whence they could see without being seen.

Among the topmost branches of this tree the crows perched, and their restless eyes wandered over the landscape in all directions. They did not lose sight, however, of everything that occurred on the farm. Evidently something of interest was about to take place, for the crows were very uneasy. For a short time they would sit looking about them in silence, when all at once one of them would give a sudden caw, which the other immediately answered, and then both cawed together excitedly.

A large hen-house stood near by, and

toward this the attention of the restless crows was often directed. The hens, too, were collected in groups in the hen-yard, and incessantly cackling, the feathers about their necks bristling with excitement, as if some danger were impending. Whatever it was that gave them such uneasiness must in some way have been connected with the hen-house itself, for the disturbed hens cast frequent glances under the building, as if some enemy were concealed there.

The crows, too, looked frequently in the same direction, as if they expected something to occur in that quarter.

At last one of the crows, glancing across the field, gave a sudden caw, and his companion answered at once. Both evidently talked it over, then suddenly became silent, their eyes fixed intently on a dark object moving cautiously along the border of the stream. It was the same sluggish stream that flowed by the abode of old Rough, and the dark object approaching was no other than the old miser himself.

Old Rough proceeded very cautiously as he approached the farm building. Often he paused, and sitting on his haunches, looked anxiously about, as if he were in a locality with which he was not familiar, and where he must be on the alert. As he sat up to take these observations, his sharp eyes glanced suspiciously about, and his long nose twitched nervously. Satisfied that all was safe, he resumed his journey in the same cautious manner, taking care to keep on the edge of the stream, as if to take refuge there in case of a surprise.

When opposite the out-buildings of the farm, he left the stream, and proceeded in the same wary manner in the direction of the hen-house.

When the two young crows, who had watched the old water-rat's movements with such interest, saw him approaching the hen-house, they quietly left their hiding-place, and flew off with as little noise as possible, as if to escape the old miser's notice.

At first the two crows flew toward the woods, and were soon lost among the thick forest-trees; but when out of sight of the farm, they struck out in the direction whence old Rough had appeared, and before long found themselves in the neighborhood of the old water-rat's dwelling.

Evidently the plans of the young crows were arranged between them, for one of them alighted on the tall tree that grew near by, while the other at once proceeded to the old rat's home. After delivering himself of several caws of derision, he recited the following verse: —

> "There was once a crabbed old miser,
> Who thought no one could be wiser;
> But his wife once he told,
> By two crows he 'd been sold,
> Which did n't seem much to surprise her."

No sooner had the crow ended than his words had the desired effect of bringing Ruffina to the door, her long nose fairly quivering with excitement, and her eyes glaring angrily on the impudent young crow.

"Be off, you impertinent fellow!" squeaked Ruffina, angrily; "you shall pay for this when my husband returns!"

"Pray don't tell him," replied the crow, pretending to shake with fear; "he might hurt us, you know."

"You deserve to have your neck wrung!" retorted Ruffina; "and if Rough does n't do it, *I* will."

The only response from the crow was a burst of laughter, that, as he fully intended it should, exasperated the old rat more than anything he could have done.

At this fresh insult, Ruffina lost the small remnant of self-control she possessed, and charged on the crow, who walked rapidly off, pursued by the enraged water-rat.

No sooner had Ruffina left her dwelling than the crow who had remained on the tree flew quickly down and disappeared inside the old miser's abode.

All this time Ruffina was pursuing the other crow, who walked and flew along the ground, allowing himself to be nearly caught, and then, with a few flaps of his strong wings, easily keeping out of the way.

It was an easy matter for the active young crow to elude the grasp of the old water-rat; and exceedingly exasperating for her was it to feel him at one moment within reach of her paw, and the next, to see him, with a single stroke of his wings, pass beyond her reach. This game was continued until the crow saw his brother emerge from the old miser's dwelling, with a fine piece of pork-rind in his bill. As soon as he saw this, he flew upon a large stone, and flapping his wings triumphantly, cawed out, —

"Pray give our regards to the old gentleman, and tell him we thought we'd save him the trouble of bringing the pork-rind to us, so we came for it ourselves." With these words he rejoined his brother, and both flew off to the woods, to enjoy in privacy the prize they had obtained so easily.

We will leave the young crows perched on a tree in the midst of the woods, quarrelling over their ill-gotten treasure, and follow the fortunes of old Rough.

We left the old miser at the moment when he had quitted the border of the stream, and had started in the direction of the farm-buildings. Directly toward the hen-house the water-rat made his way, stopping more frequently as he neared it, looking anxiously about him, and evidently prepared to run back at a moment's notice.

As old Rough neared the building, the timid hens retreated to the extreme end of their yard, their necks stretched to their fullest extent, their feathers ruffled with excitement, and constantly uttering cries of terror.

When he reached the hen-house yard, the water-rat stood on his hind legs, and resting his forepaws on the ledge of the building, gazed at the terrified creatures within with a gratified expression on his wicked old features. At this horrible apparition, the poor hens became still more frightened, and gave vent to their alarm in loud and shrill screams.

"Not to-day, my friends, — I have another engagement; but I will visit you later," said the old rat, with an unpleasant leer on his ugly features; and dropping to the ground, he proceeded to the hen-house itself, and paused before it.

"'T was very fortunate for me that the crows, in their stupidity, told me where Bobtilla had moved, for I should never have thought of looking here for her. Stupid fellows, those crows! they don't know old Rough very well, or they would n't have expected to get the sheep's pluck and pork-rind. Very shrewd in Bobtilla to choose this place. She never thought of it herself, that is certain; those smart squirrels must have put her up to it."

The old miser peered cautiously about the foundation of the hen-house. It was built of large stones loosely fitted together, which served as a support for the wooden structure. After a careful survey, old Rough discovered what was evidently a mouse-hole, and he looked cautiously in. Nothing could he see or hear, and he scraped the earth away, in order to enlarge the opening. He found nothing inside, however, but a mouse-nest that had been long deserted; so he continued his search.

Nothing could the old rat discover that resembled the place the crows had described as Bobtilla's new residence. At last, when he was becoming convinced that this must have been a trick of the mischievous crows to mislead him, he observed what seemed to be a rat-hole in one corner of the wall.

"Why did n't I see that before?" said old Rough to himself; "they said she had taken possession of an empty rat-hole, and just like the shiftless creature, too, it is. However, she shall pay for keeping me waiting so long;" and very cautiously the old miser approached the entrance and looked in.

"I could probably squeeze myself in," thought old Rough, "but it would be rather close quarters for one of my size to turn around in, so I 'll make her come out.— Bobtilla," he called sternly, "I have something to say to you."

No response came to his call, and he inclined his ear to the hole. He could distinctly hear somebody moving about inside, and he smiled at the thought of the treat in store for him.

"Bobtilla, I say!" called the old miser again; "will you come out, or do you prefer to have me come in?"

No reply came to this second call, except a slight rustling from within.

"I see you, madam," called out the old rat, looking into the dark opening; "I advise you to come out at once, or I shall come and fetch you. It will be all the same to me, but perhaps not quite so agreeable to you."

In reply, a shrill little voice was heard from within: "Come in! here I am."

Enraged at this insolence, the old water-rat began to dig away the earth from the entrance to what he supposed was the field-mouse's abode; but suddenly he stopped in his work, and gave a shrill squeal of terror;

for instead of the timid little Bobtilla whom he intended to torture, a slender animal with long, brownish fur came wriggling fiercely toward him. It was the deadliest enemy of the rat tribe, the weasel, and never in all his life had old Rough found himself in such a dangerous situation.

Casting a terrified glance about him for a refuge, the old water-rat darted between the stones that formed the foundation of the hen-house, and found himself in the open space under the floor of the building.

As he glanced about him in hope of discovering some loop-hole for escape, old Rough saw the long, flexible body of the weasel wriggling through the same passage by which he had come, his sharp eyes following him with an expression of intense ferocity.

No greater terror could the wicked old water-rat have inspired in poor timid Bobtilla than that he now felt for the powerful weasel, and for one single instant old Rough stood irresolute; but the long lithe body of the weasel was wriggling nearer and nearer, and the water-rat made a desperate rush for a hole in one corner. He was through in an instant, and stood panting in a dark passage-way that was, or had once been, the home of some rat. Several smaller passage-ways led in different directions, and old Rough rushed into the one nearest him. Groping his way blindly, he soon found himself in a large apartment.

No living creatures were to be seen, but the dry leaves and rags and paper in one corner evidently had recently served as a bed for some one; and the old rat shuddered as he descried in one corner the lifeless body of a mouse, whose life-blood had evidently been recently drawn.

The old rat shook with terror as the horrible thought dawned on him that he had hit upon the abode of the ferocious creature from whom he was trying to escape. Cruel and contemptible as was the old miser's character, he was not lacking in physical courage; and turning his face toward the various entrances that opened from the cavern, he resolved to make a bold stand for his life, and awaited breathlessly the appearance of his enemy, for he knew he would lose no time in following him.

Old Rough had not long to wait; but every moment seemed an age as his sharp eyes glanced from one to another of the several openings. Before long, his keen ears detected a slight noise, and he knew well what it meant. The weasel was approaching, — but by which entrance? With a fast-beating heart, old Rough waited until the gleaming teeth of his relentless enemy appeared, and then, with all speed, the desperate water-rat darted into another of the passages.

Could he have made a mistake, and chosen a passage that had no exit at the other end?   Old Rough began to fear that such was the case, for it seemed to him, in his agony, as if the darkness grew more dense; and with horror he perceived that the passage grew more and more narrow, until he was forced, in places, to dig with all the desperation of despair a space large enough for his huge body to pass.

So slow had the old miser's progress become that he lost much time, and he realized despairingly that his pursuer was steadily gaining on him; for the weasel, with his long and flexible body, could easily slip through crevices too small for the bulky form of the old water-rat.

Yes, the weasel was gaining on him! The old rat, panting from terror and prodigious exertions, felt that his enemy was close behind, and every minute expected to feel those sharp teeth fasten on his back; but the old miser was resolved to sell his life as dearly as possible, and making a gigantic effort he tore away a projection of earth that obstructed his path, and found, to his great relief, that the passage-way once more grew wide.

11

"And the old miser, who now felt that the decisive moment had
arrived, turned and faced his enemy."

CHAPTER XI.

THE COMBAT.

THE path was indeed much wider, and
the old water-rat took courage, for he
knew from experience that these passage-
ways always grow wide as they approach
the exit. If he could but escape from this
subterranean abode, he felt there was a
chance for him, for he could when out-

side at least face his enemy and make a fight for his life.

The weasel was still close behind; but now that the water-rat had once more a wide passage-way, he could make more progress, and he bounded rapidly forward. Realizing so fully his dangerous position, his silent enemy pursuing him relentlessly and surely, not one pang of conscience smote him for the many times he had put others in the same danger the weasel now placed him. If he had reflected on the matter at all, he would have resolved to make others suffer, in the future, what he was now suffering; for not one ray of pity was in the old miser's heart. Self, alone, had always been the one purpose of his life, and always would be, as long as life remained to him.

No such reflections, however, disturbed the old water-rat's mind; his sole aim was to escape this ferocious enemy, that was so silently pursuing him. With a bound of his wicked old heart, he descried a faint ray of light in the distance, and, filled with new courage, redoubled his efforts.

His unusual exertion had told heavily on the old water-rat, and in spite of his efforts the steady progress of the weasel, who was as fresh as when he started, enabled him to gain on the exhausted rat. As the latter emerged once more into the open space under the floor of the hen-house, the weasel was close upon him, and the old miser, who now felt that the decisive moment had arrived, turned and faced his enemy.

The deadly contest began in earnest. The weasel was bent on fastening his long, sharp teeth in the old water-rat's neck, that he might drain his blood, and the old rat, with his sharp teeth and strong paws, endeavored to keep him at bay.

The old water-rat's strength was fast giving way, however. Almost sightless from the weakness that came so fast upon him, and faint from loss of blood that flowed from the wounds inflicted by the sharp teeth of his enemy, he knew that a few moments must decide his fate. At last he realized that the decisive moment had indeed come, as his now feeble paws could no longer keep back the strong weasel; and as he felt the last remnant of strength depart, and saw his enemy preparing for his final grip, squeal after squeal of agony issued from his throat. So penetrating were they in their shrillness that even the fierce weasel arrested the final blow, and paused for an instant.

During this instant a loud clamor arose from the terrified hens assembled in the corner of the hen-yard, and this was immediately followed by the loud barking of a little terrier, who at once rushed in the direction whence the squeals of the water-rat issued, and pushed his inquisitive nose in between the crevices of the stones, while with his strong little paws he set to work to enlarge an opening. At the same instant, too, the voice of the farmer was heard directly behind the terrier, saying, as he dislodged a large stone: " Go in and find 'em, old boy, — go in and find 'em!"

Into the breach sprang the excited terrier, and away sped the weasel back to the same retreat from which he had first emerged; and while the terrier was scratching and snuffing at the opening, the wounded water-rat, unnoticed by the eager terrier, managed to drag his exhausted body to the wall, and emerged on the outside of the hen-house.

Weary and wounded as the old miser was, he succeeded in reaching a pile of boards that stood behind the barns, and crawling beneath them threw himself down on the ground thoroughly exhausted, and lay motionless. If the weasel could have discovered him now, he might have despatched him without any resistance on the old rat's part.

Long did old Rough lie under the pile of boards, until day lengthened into twilight, and twilight deepened into night; and then, when all was still and dark, the old miser arose on his stiff legs and crawled slowly forth from his hiding-place. Before him lay the stream which had so often risen to his mind as he lay hot and aching under the pile of boards, and toward it he now directed his steps,— not with the agility and alertness with which he had passed over the same ground a few hours before, but slowly and listlessly, dragging along his aching body.

At last the soft mud on the bank of the brook was reached, and the weary old miser slid into the turbid stream, sighing with re-lief as the cool water came into contact with his feverish body.

Refreshing and invigorating was the old water-rat's native element, and under its soothing and healing influence he felt a portion of his old strength gradually coming back to him. At first he floated slowly along, abandoning himself to the pleasing sensations the cool water afforded him; by degrees he increased his progress, swimming with ease, and before long stopped before his own door. Not a feeling of gratitude or joy at having had his life so mercifully and unexpectedly preserved did the sordid old miser feel, but he dragged his wounded body into his den, and with an angry squeak aroused Ruffina from slumber.

"Dear me, Rough!" exclaimed his wife, who was thus suddenly disturbed in her dreams, "what a long time you've been gone. I thought something must have happened to you."

"Much it would trouble you," muttered the old rat. "Come, bustle around and bring me something to eat, for I'm precious weak from loss of blood."

"Good gracious!" squealed Ruffina, "what have you been about? Why, you are bitten all to pieces. You don't mean to say those horrid crows did that?"

"Stop that noise, and don't be a fool,—if you can help it. How do you suppose crows could give me such wounds as these?"

"Who did, then?" asked his wife, examining the sharp cuts about his neck and face, from which the blood still oozed.

"No matter who it was. You just bustle around and bring me some of that pork-rind I brought home the other day,—that will set me up quicker than anything else."

"There is n't any," answered Ruffina, in a faint voice.

"What!" snarled the old miser. "No pork? What do you mean?"

"It 's been stolen," explained his wife, trembling under her lord's angry glances; "but I could n't help it. *I* was n't to blame."

"You 've eaten it up, you thief!" cried

the old miser, in a rage. "How dared you, when I told you not so much as to look at it?"

"Indeed, I did n't touch it," explained his wife, timidly; "I put it away in one corner, for fear I might be tempted to taste it; but he found it and carried it off."

"*He?* Whom do you mean by *he*, you exasperating idiot? Why can't you explain yourself properly? You are at no loss for words when you ought to keep still."

Thus adjured, Ruffina related the visit of the two young crows, and explained how one had enticed her away from the house, while the other entered it and stole the pork-rind, and she ended by repeating the verse the crow had addressed to her.

His wife's account of the theft seemed sufficiently plausible to the miser, and he now realized the extent of the young crows' treachery. That they had purposely led him to the weasel's abode, thinking he would never return thence, he did not for a moment doubt, and he resolved to inflict sure and summary vengeance upon them in return.

Long after his wife was sleeping soundly, did the old water-rat lie awake, concocting plans to carry out his revenge, not only on the impudent young crows, but also on the defenceless Bobtilla and the officious chipmunks who had interfered in his plans. After long thought, a scheme occurred to him which made him smile grimly to himself, and mutter, — "It may be long before I can accomplish it, but I will bide my time."

This thought was so gratifying that the old water-rat at once betook himself to bed, and soon fell into a deep and refreshing slumber.

We will leave old Rough to enjoy his much needed rest, and follow the adventures of other friends.

The Widow O'Warty was quite disconcerted for a time at the trick played upon her by the saucy crows; but she was too good-natured to bear resentment long, and soon laughed at the recollection of the event.

"It's meself that injoyed the pleasure of a serenade that was intinded for another," she said to herself; "an' afther all, there's no harrm done. It's a rale gintleman is Johnny the basso, an' a foine singer, an' it's pl'ased I should account meself to continue his acquaintance."

So a few days later, when the widow met the basso in the meadow, she accosted him graciously.

"It's pl'ased I am to see ye; an' it's proud I should account meself to see you at me reciption the evening," said the smiling widow.

"You do me great honor, Madame La Warty," replied the basso, courteously; "at what hour will Madame permit me to visit her?"

"Whin the jew is on the grass and the moon is up," said the widow, "the company will assimble forninst me dwilling. Is it the swate singer Signor Trillo ye have mit?"

"No, I have not had the *plaisir* tó meet him," answered the basso, somewhat haughtily; for the name suggested a possible rival.

"Is that the troot?" asked the widow. "It's surprised I am to hear the same. The gintleman houlds a high station in his own counthry; indade, I'm tould he's nixt removed from the king. It's many the reciptions an' kittle-dhrums an' shmoke-talks the 'tin million' have given him, an' indade it's surprised I am yees have niver mit. Two such swate singers should become known to each ither, an' it's meself that will have the pl'isure of introjucing yees. It's foine the v'ices of yees will blind togither, for it's a swate tenor the signor possesses."

"I do not wish to sing wiz zee tenor, Madame La Warty," replied the basso, excitedly. "I 'ate ze tenor voice. He squeal, he know not what musique is. Zee great basso-profundo will not sing wiz your tenor, Madame."

"Oh, no! you are mistaken," answered the widow, good-naturedly; "the signor does not squeal; it is a full rich v'ice himself has, — not sich a foine v'ice as yourself, to be sure," added the widow, quickly, who saw the effect of her injudicious praise of the tenor, and who wished to retain the favor of the sensitive basso, "but a swate v'ice for a *tenor*, av coorse, I m'ane."

The feeling of jealousy that had taken possession of the basso's breast during the widow's praise of the tenor, made his throat swell and vibrate with the strength of the emotion that raged within him; but the effect of her last words caused the tumult within him to subside, and with an effort he regained his usual composure.

"I sall have zee *honneur* to wait on Madame La Warty zis evening," replied the basso, politely. "I will make my adieu to Madame if she will permit, as I have an appointment to meet."

"Who is zis tenor, zis Signor Trillo?" said the basso to himself. "I do not believe zat he is one great noble. I do not believe zat he can sing; but I will see him, — I will laugh at zis tenor when he goes to sing! I, zee great basso-profundo, will sing so loud zat zey sall not hear one tone from zis squealing pig."

"The Widow O'Warty's reception."

CHAPTER XII.

THE WIDOW O'WARTY'S RECEPTION.

THE hour for the Widow O'Warty's reception was approaching, and everything seemed favorable for a happy evening. The sun disappeared in the west, and the golden and red-tinted clouds reflected his parting rays.   These deepened into a violet hue, as twilight stole gradually on, and then a soft gray light fell over all.

This is the hour dear to all the little animals that inhabit the woods and fields. They seem to fear the brilliant daylight, and their timid natures grow bolder as night steals on.

At this hour the cheerful crickets sing out more cheerfully and boldly, the shy tree-toads pipe their shrill song, and from every ditch and pond arise the melancholy tones of the emotional frog, the far-reaching tenor and the resounding bass.

In the depths of the wood rings out more often the cheerful chirrup of the shy squirrel; the hedge-hog squeaks, and the little mice scurry along the ground. All of these sounds were heard on the evening of the Widow O'Warty's reception, and as night came on these voices increased.

Then, when the twilight disappeared and all grew dark, out came the fire-flies, floating over the meadow, and often soaring over the tallest trees, every motion of their gauzy wings displaying the brilliant strips of greenish light on their little bodies.

The glow-worms, too, wriggled their shining bodies through the grass, doing their best to light on their way the Widow O'Warty's guests.

The hostess herself sat in front of her dwelling, her affable countenance wreathed in smiles, as she welcomed each guest. A lawn-party it must be, for the widow's house was too dark and cramped to contain the hosts of friends her hospitality included.

Johnny the basso was one of the first to arrive, and, as he sat beside the hostess, she found time, between the arrivals, to acquaint him with the characters of her guests.

"It's a furriner ye are, an' it's meself that will acquaint ye wid the ways of me fri'nds," she explained.

A light green katydid, accompanied by her pale and delicate looking son, were seen approaching.

"Sure, an' if me two eyes do not dec'ave me, that swate cratur Katrina Diddo an' her. remarkable son are appearing to me view. Good evening, Ma'arm," continued the hostess, as the two approached. "It's proud I account meself to rec'ave yees."

"Thanks," murmured the katydid, with her head poised on one side, and her full eyes gazing with a rapt expression far over the Widow O'Warty's head into vacancy. "How extremely kind of you to draw us out this marvellous evening, when each slender blade of grass and each tiny leaflet is bathed in translucent dew, and the spirit of inspiration hovers above us, earth creatures as we are;" and the speaker heaved a sigh as she closed her eyes dreamily.

"It's *intinse* Katrina is," whispered the

widow to the basso; "an' how is the swate b'y, ma'am," she added, to the poetic katy-did, whose dreamy eyes still looked far away into space.

"Well, my dear Widow. Excelsior is as well as one can be, who hears the voice of genius forever calling him to higher things, and to deeds where we, poor earth-worms as we are, cannot follow him, — that cease-less call, as the ocean beats his great heart out against a giant wall. Ah me! what is life!"

"Ye may well remark it," answered the widow; "it 's a mystery, is life, an' that 's the troot."

"You know it? You feel it too?" ex-claimed Katrina, with a sudden burst of intensity. "Oh! the crushing weight of that thought to a soaring human soul!"

With a deep sigh the poetess passed on, followed closely by her talented son.

"Zis grande poetess, I perceive she have

one foreign name; I taught she was American," remarked the basso, as the pair disappeared.

"It's American hersilf is," replied the widow, confidentially, "an' it's Katy Did her name is; but whin it's famous she became, she changed the name of her, Katy did, as was r'asonable. It's one of the 'tin million' Katy is," added the widow, in a whisper.

The poetess's son, Excelsior, had not spoken a word, but had gazed about him in an abstracted manner during the conversation between his mother and the Widow O'Warty, not evincing by a look or sign that he had understood the conversation.

"What's zee matter wiz zat *garçon?*" asked the basso, who had been a silent observer.

"Ye may will ask fwhat's the matter wid the gossoon; an' it's mesilf that's not able to acquaint you wid his complaint," replied the widow; "but I suspicion that it's on account of the head of him being too large for the body of him."

"What does he do, this *spirituel garçon?* Does he make poetry like his talented mamma?"

"Indade an' he does no sich a thing," replied the widow, in a tone that expressed resentment at the question. "There is not body enough to contain the brain av him in the furst place; an' thin it's such a d'ale of thinking the cratur kapes up that there's no vint for the same, an' the thoughts they kape revolving trou' the brain av him, till I'm tauld there's great danger av an ixplosion."

"I am sorry for zis *pauvre garçon,*" replied the basso; and he once more watched with interest the poetess and her remarkable son, who was unable to give expression to the great thoughts that seethed through his gigantic brain.

"Della bella Wartyo," cried a high tenor voice, as a tree-toad appeared.

"Is it yourself, Signor Trillo?" answered the widow, cordially. "It's rej'iced to see ye I am. I was afeard we should lose the pl'isure of your company this evening."

"A million thanks," replied the tenor, effusively; "Madame is too gracious."

"I take pl'isure, Signor, in presinting to ye Johnny the basso, the swatest of singers, yourself ixcipted," said the widow, graciously.

Johnny the basso darted a scrutinizing glance at the tenor, for a secret misgiving seized him. Could this tenor be the identical one who had stolen from him the affection of the little brown frog? It might be so, — that this foreigner, said to be of noble birth, so much courted and fêted by the "ten million" on account of the high position he was supposed to hold in his native land, had won the fancy of the fair brown frog. But he would not be precipitate, he would watch this tenor; and if his suspicions were verified, then let the tenor look to his safety!

The tenor evidently was not disturbed by any such emotions as agitated the great basso, and he greeted the latter in so unembarrassed a manner, that the basso felt obliged to conceal his suspicions as well as possible, and wait for future developments.

"It's a po'me Katrina Diddo will be afther reciting to us," said the widow, as the poetess came forward, and fixing her eyes on the full moon that stood overhead, gazed at it awhile in silence. Then, while the other guests waited breathlessly for the inspiration that she seemed invoking from that brilliant orb, Katrina, still gazing upward, recited the following lines: —

> "Sunflower of the sky,
>   Oh! why
> Floatest thou
>   On high?

> "The lily lovest thou?
>   Now, now,
> To her descends
>   Thy vow.

> "Clothed in celestial light,
>   Bright, bright,
>   Into her flower-heart,
>   It flows at night."

"How exquisite!" murmured an ecstatic young grasshopper, who had gazed enraptured on the ardent poetess; "methinks I faint with the sweet oppression."

"Ye may will faint, that's a fact!" replied the Widow O'Warty. "Will ye recite that iligant thing, 'Among the Daffodils'? I'm tauld it's accounted the finest po'me ye've proju'ced yit."

Whereupon the poetess, fixing her eyes on vacancy, recited the following verses:—

> "Among the daffodils,
>   Ah me! so lonesome!
>   Bending toward flowing rills,
>   Ah me! so lonesome!
>   Heart, cease thy beating,
>   Ah me! so lonesome!
>   Hear lambkin bleating,
>   Ah me! so lonesome!
>
> "Lambkin and daffodils,
>   Lonesome, so lonesome!
>   Ye flowerets, ye wandering rills,
>   Lonesome, so lonesome!

> Lamb, to thy mother flee,
> No longer lonesome,
> Mated my heart shall be,
> No longer lonesome."

"An' now will ye give us the pl'isure of a song, Signor Trillo?" asked the hostess, when the enthusiasm that followed the poem had died away.

The tenor, in his high voice, responded with the following ditty:—

> "Oh! say, have you heard,
> From yonder bog,
> The merry refrain
> Of the little brown frog?
>
> "When the moon shineth down
> On streamlet and rill,
> You may hear in the fields,
> The brown frog's trill.
>
> "And all the night long.
> And through the day,
> The little brown frog
> Is singing away,
>
> "Till my heart has grown sad
> From the love I bring her,
> And all for the sake
> Of the little brown singer."

During the song, the basso felt his emotion overpowering him, and at its conclusion he hopped up to the singer and exclaimed fiercely, —

"I wish to know, sair, who is zis leetle brown frog of whom you sing?"

The tenor turned, and gazed in astonishment on the excited countenance of the disturbed basso.

"I don't fancy fat bassos, replied the saucy Brownella, hopping to the tenor's side."

CHAPTER XIII.

THE RIVALS.

"I DID not mention the name of the little brown frog," answered Signor Trillo, haughtily.

"But I desire to know zee name of zee leetle brown frog, Monsieur," persisted the excited basso. "I myself know one leetle brown frog, and I wish to know zee name of her of whom you sing."

"That is my concern alone," replied the tenor, in the same haughty manner. "The name of her whose beauty I sing shall remain deeply written on my heart, and the wealth of the world would not tempt me to disclose it."

"What depth of soul!" softly murmured Katrina, "what delicacy of feeling!" and all the assembled guests gazed admiringly on the noble-spirited tenor.

"But you *sall* disclose zee name of zee leetle brown frog!" exclaimed the basso, fiercely. "I seek one leetle brown frog, and I suspect, Monsieur, zat zis is zee one. On your *honneur*, I demand zee name of zee leetle brown frog."

"The honor of the fair sex is dearer to me than my own," answered the tenor, "and I refuse to disclose the name of her whose praises I sing."

A murmur ran through the assembly at these chivalrous words, — the crickets and grasshoppers boldly sang out their admiration, the frogs and toads croaked approval, the fire-flies rushed excitedly about, while the susceptible Katrina gave utterance to several sighs, as she murmured, —

"What nobility of thought! what tenacity of purpose! Happy little brown frog, to inspire such wealth of affection in so intense a nature!"

As the admiration of the tenor increased, disapproval of the basso's conduct grew in proportion, and severe were the indignant glances cast upon him.

"I say to you zat you *have* no *honneur!* I say to you zat you are no noble in your native land! I say to you zat you are no Italien! I say to you zat you are one Yankee! I say to you zat you are one coward and one *imposteur!*" And the excitable basso paused, quite out of breath.

For an instant after these audacious words there was a pause; but by degrees the buzz of the assembled guests grew louder and louder, until not a sound could be heard above the angry hum. All their indignation was centered on the bold basso, who had dared to insult the noble signor who held such a high position in his native land.

"You shall retract your words, sir!" said the signor, when the voices of his admirers had subsided sufficiently to allow him to be heard. "You shall not insult a tree-toad of noble birth with impunity! You shall answer for this insult."

"I say to you once more zat you are *not* of noble birth,—zat you are one Yankee *imposteur*, sair! You know well zat zee peoples in zis land feel zemselves proud to make zee acquaintance of zee great Italien noble; zat when he go to zem and say: 'Behold me, I have no food to eat; it is not possible for so great a noble as I to work for my food; will you zee goodness have to give me from your abundance till I hear from my noble friends in Italy?' zen all zee peoples feel their-selves proud to give to zee noble foreigner. Zat is how it is, I know it; and I say zat you are one *imposteur*, sair, and I challenge you to deny it, sair!"

"What's the use of all this quarrell-ing?" cried a gay voice, and a sprightly young brown frog hopped between the two disputants, and looked pertly about her.

"Brownella!" exclaimed the basso in astonishment. "Do I see you at last?"

"I suppose you do, if you loòk this way," answered Brownella, saucily.

"The lady shall decide the matter," said Signor Trillo.

"Brownella, have you forgotten the vows we plighted, the sonnets I have sung beneath your window?" asked the basso, tenderly.

"Oh, bother!" ejaculated Brownella, with a coquettish toss of the head.

"Have you forgotten how I, zee greatest basso-profundo on zee earth, have sat night after night in zee cold, wet bog, chanting your praises? Have you no remembrance of zis, I ask?"

"I told you our voices did n't blend well," replied Brownella, pertly. "How absurd for a soprano and basso-profundo to try to sing together! We should only make a spectacle of ourselves."

"If zee hearts blend, what matter about zee voices?" asked the basso, fondly.

"I never yet made an object of myself, and I don't intend to begin now," answered Brownella, saucily.

"Will you choose, Brownella, between this basso and me?" asked the tenor, who had manifested great satisfaction in the brown frog's replies to the basso. "Which shall it be, this fat basso, or the tenor with the noble pedigree?"

"I don't fancy fat bassos," replied the saucy Brownella, hopping to the tenor's side, while all the assembled guests sent up a hum of approval.

There was nothing left for the basso but to accept his disappointment as he best could, and with great ferocity he said to the tenor, "You sall have occasion to show if you are one coward. I sall have zee pleasure to meet you, Monsieur, to-morrow evening in zee meadow by zee bog."

"I shall be there without fail," replied the tenor, haughtily; and abruptly saluting the hostess, the basso hopped angrily away.

The next night, as soon as the moon appeared, the basso proceeded to the bog in the meadow, to meet, in mortal combat, the tenor who had so deeply insulted him. Toward the faithless Brownella, he seemed to bear no resentment, concentrating all his wrath on the foreign singer who had stolen from him the affections of the little brown frog.

Not long did the basso sit on the moist edge of the bog before the guests who had assembled the evening before at the Widow O'Warty's reception began to arrive, all eager to witness the contest between the two great singers.

The poetical Katrina and the talented Excelsior were among the early arrivals, the poetess improving the time that elapsed before the arrival of the tenor in composing a sonnet to the genius of her remarkable son.

Why did not the tenor appear? What could his absence mean? The guests were beginning to ask themselves these questions, as time went on and the tenor failed to appear.

Groups of frogs were earnestly discussing

the merits of the two combatants, some offering wagers as to the result of the contest; here and there bands of crickets and grasshoppers were talking over the quarrel of the evening before in their shrill voices; and the fire-flies darted about impetuously, often soaring far out of sight, and always returning with the information that the tenor was nowhere to be seen.

At last whispers were heard suggesting that perhaps after all the tenor would not appear; that he was purposely keeping away.

All this time the basso sat silently on the margin of the bog, glaring fiercely about him in every direction, hoping to catch sight of his adversary, — silent except for an occasional deep-voiced croak expressive of wrath.

As the moon rose higher into the sky, and star after star came out, and still the tenor did not appear, the hum of voices grew louder, and took on an angry tone; and as is often the case with impulsive natures, the very ones who had the evening before been the most enthusiastic over the Italian tenor, now were the first to suspect him of intentionally staying away, and to accuse him of cowardice.

The boldness of the bull-frog, as he sat silently and ferociously awaiting his rival's coming, began to make an impression in his favor; and before long, audible remarks disparaging the tenor were heard.

At this point, a fine large fire-fly was seen flying rapidly toward the company, and when he reached them, he sank exhausted on the moist grass that surrounded the bog. All looked eagerly toward him, for they knew he had news to tell them. As soon as he recovered his breath sufficiently to speak, he said,—

"It's of no use waiting any longer; he is n't coming."

"Where is he?" was asked on all sides.

"Taken himself off, nobody knows where," answered the fire-fly, as well as he could for want of breath.

"To think of the times I've hunted food for the lazy thing!" exclaimed a toad, angrily.

"And I too!" was heard from many voices.

"An' think on the iligant reciption meself gave in his honor!" exclaimed the Widow O'Warty.

"And the sonnets I've dedicated to him!" murmured Katrina Diddo, dejectedly.

"It's meself that always suspected he was dec'aving us," said the widow.

"So I have always said," remarked a stout frog, who had shortly before been one of the tenor's most ardent admirers. "I've always said he'd turn out to be a fraud, and now I hope you'll believe me."

"The airs the cratur put on!" said the

Widow O'Warty. "It's aisy to spake about the foine relations of him whin it's so far removed they are."

"And to think of the poor little brown frog!" exclaimed another; "how he has deceived her!"

All the company, who so short a time before were enthusiastic on the subject of the noble foreigner, were now just as ready to denounce him.

All this time the bull-frog, who had been so imposed upon, had remained too deeply absorbed in his own wrongs to attend to the remarks of the company.

"Faith, an' it's sorry for ye I am, Johnny," said the good-hearted widow, as the basso was about to take his departure. "He's a villain, is Trillo, an' that's the troot."

"I knew it would turn out this way," remarked to the basso the stout frog who had before spoken. "It won't do to trust these foreigners too far. I knew you were right, when you exposed him yesterday."

"So did I," said another of Signor Trillo's former admirers.

"I sank you for your very kind opinions," responded the basso, politely; "but you will pardon me if I say zat it is razer late to express zese good opinions. If I do not deceive myself, it was quite otherwise yesterday;" and with a courteous but frigid salutation, Johnny the basso dived into the pool, and was not seen until he reappeared on the other side, when he uttered a loud and agonizing "a-hung!"

The company looked at one another in astonishment at the cool reception their expressions of sympathy had met with from the great singer, and several murmured disapproval. The Widow O'Warty, whose good-nature always asserted itself, was the first to recover herself.

"It's disapp'inted he is, an' no wonder.

An' his thrubbles are not over yet, I'm thinking, for a dec'ateful cratur is that Brownella; an' now that Trillo has taken his departure, it's once more sthriving to obtain the affections of poor Johnny she'll be."

"It's my opinion she'll not succeed," observed a young frog. "I think he's tired of her long ago, and I'm sure there are plenty more attractive than that little dark-skinned Brownella."

"She was always a saucy thing," said the stout frog. "I always told my daughters to have nothing to do with her."

"She had betther kape her spickled face to home, or it's a warm reception the saucy cratur will find here," remarked the widow. "But what in the world is the matter, that ye must needs frighten a body like that?" she continued, as a bat flew so closely to her, and with so little noise, that she started back in alarm. "Oh! it's yourself, is it, Misther Flipwing? An' fwhat in the world's name is the matther?"

"Have you heard the news?" Flipwing asked, as he clung to the trunk of a tree in his favorite position, head downward.

"What news do ye m'ane? Is it that the raskill Trillo has absconded, afther recaving the attintions of the 'tin million?' Yis, we've heard it; an' it's small astonishment the news gave meself, for it's meself that suspicted from the first that he was a dec'aver."

"No, I don't mean that," replied the bat. "I mean about Squirrello's youngster, you know."

"No, I do not know," said the widow, eagerly. "Will ye pl'ase to ixplain yourself, and acquaint us wid the news!"

"Well, then," responded Flipwing, "Squirrello's youngest has disappeared; either strayed away and got lost, or been entrapped. *I*'m in favor of the latter theory."

"The purty little thing, wid the soft and bushy tail of him!" exclaimed the widow; "it's sorry for him I am."

"How did it happen?" demanded many voices.

Flipwing could not satisfy their curiosity. He could only tell them that the little squirrel had suddenly disappeared; that his parents had searched everywhere in vain for him, and that they were almost distracted with grief at their loss.

This news all heard with regret, and each determined to do his best to discover the fate of the lost squirrel.

"Yees have all heard of the sarvices Misther Flipwing has rendered on former occasions," observed the widow; "an' wid his hilp we'll find the poor b'y."

CHAPTER XIV.

FLUFF IS LOST.

THE news brought by the bat Flipwing
was correct,— the youngest of the
squirrel family, little Fluff, was indeed missing, and great was the distress of his family
in consequence. The first day of freedom,
— that on which the two young crows had
discovered the new dwellings of the field-

mouse and squirrels, when the young squirrels had ventured out alone for the first time in their lives, — proved to be a most disastrous event, for it awoke in their young natures a taste for adventure that was most dangerous.

So delightful was this new experience, that it became the custom of the young squirrels daily, in the absence of their parents, to venture out boldly, and enjoy the freedom of the woods. Bobtilla's children, possessing more timid natures, dared not join their neighbors in their adventures, but remained quietly at home; while their fearless playmates, made confident by the seclusion and solitude about them, became constantly bolder, and each day ventured farther out.

Such a vigilant old fellow as the miser Rough, who was now bent on discovering the new retreat of his enemies, as he chose to consider the harmless little field-mouse and squirrels, could not fail before long to find them out.

One day, hidden behind a moss-covered stump, old Rough discovered the young squirrels frisking merrily about among the trees and over the rocks; and he soon learned that it was the habit of these active young creatures to venture out daily, as soon as their parents had departed in search of food, and pursue their innocent gambols.

Then did the old water-rat set his wicked mind to work, and he soon formed a plan of revenge that afforded him perfect satisfaction.

Beneath the very stump that had served as a hiding-place whence he could watch his unsuspecting victims, he dug a long and deep den, and skilfully concealed the opening with moss and leaves. To this cavern he conducted his wife, giving her minute directions as to her part of the programme.

Ruffina promised to obey in every particular; and indeed a much bolder nature than the water-rat's submissive wife's might have quailed under the direful consequences which the old miser vowed would follow the slightest disregard of his directions.

Thus was Ruffina installed within the den, and before the opening was placed a fine acorn, while just within lay several more of unusually fine size and quality.

Meanwhile the young squirrels frisked and gambolled in their beautiful playground among the trees with not a suspicion of the plot laid for their destruction. A very venturesome squirrel was little Fluff, the youngest and most promising of the family, and his bold spirit led him into places where his more cautious brothers and sister dared not follow. His bright eyes were always spying out objects they never thought of finding, and his inquisitive little nose was constantly poking itself where it had no business to go.

The time for which old Rough had long waited at last arrived. Fluff's curious eyes espied the tempting acorn that the old miser had placed to entrap him, and in a moment he had it in his little forepaws, and his sharp teeth soon penetrated the thin shell. Selfishness was not one of Fluff's faults, and he generously divided the delicate morsel with his companions.

The acorn did not go very far, to be sure, and when the small share that fell to each was eaten, they looked at each other wistfully.

"What a pity there are no more!" said one.

"Ah, that was good," replied another, carefully examining the empty shells, in the hope that some crumbs might have been overlooked.

"There must be more," asserted Fluff, positively. "It is n't likely just one nut would be left here. It was dropped by mistake, and the rest, probably a big pile, must be near;" and Fluff's inquisitive nose and bright eyes began their investigations.

It was not long before the opening so ingeniously concealed by old Rough was brought to light, and in went Master Fluff.

"See here!" he soon called out, "what did I tell you? Here are some more of them, and you may be sure that that dark den beyond is full. Come on, and help yourselves!"

The more cautious brothers and sister, however, did not think it prudent to venture into the dark entrance to the cavern, but looked longingly in, while the bolder Fluff brought them some of the fine acorns, which, if possible, were even larger and of finer flavor than the one found outside.

These, too, were soon eaten, and then came the natural desire for more. The first peep into the dark cavern, however, had been sufficient to keep all but Fluff at a safe distance; but this venturesome young squirrel soon decided on the course he intended to pursue.

"I've made up my mind," said Fluff, boldly, "that there are plenty more acorns in that dark hole, and I'm going in."

"Going in!" exclaimed his horrified companions.

"Yes; what is there so strange in that?" laughed Fluff. "It's evident to me that that dark cave is the hiding-place of some old miser, and on the way he dropped a few of his nuts. There must be a pile of them, or he wouldn't have let such fine nuts lie there."

"Oh, don't go in!" pleaded little Flossie. "Suppose some great horrid creature with long, sharp teeth and claws lives there!"

"If I find any such thing there, I shall come right back, of course. Do you think I am so foolish as to allow myself to be nabbed?"

But Flossie's gentle little heart was not satisfied, and she continued to plead with her venturesome brother. The others, it must be confessed, did not oppose so many objections to Fluff's plans as did his tender-hearted little sister, for they greatly desired the savory nuts, and Fluff had always come off with such flying colors from the many risks he had run, that they had great confidence in his powers; so it was with some inward satisfaction that they saw him enter the passageway that led into the dark cave.

For an instant all was still, and the little squirrels waiting outside huddled together, listening breathlessly for some signal from their brother; but all at once arose in Fluff's well-known voice a sharp cry of pain, and then followed immediately repeated calls for help.

The timid creatures, terrified, scampered off as fast as they could go, leaving their courageous brother to his fate. When at a safe distance, they stopped, their hearts beating wildly and their sides palpitating, and looked timidly back at the dark cavern into which poor Fluff had disappeared.

Nothing was to be seen, and all was still; and soon came the dreadful thought, — how should they account to their parents for Fluff's absence?

Too cowardly to tell the truth, which would reveal their own disobedience, they resolved to assert boldly that Fluff had disappeared suddenly when they were at play, and they could find no traces of him.

In vain did gentle Flossie plead with them to allow her to tell the whole truth; but she was threatened with the most dreadful consequences if she did not do as they wished.

"I'll set 'Old Dead' after you, Floss, if you tell," said her oldest brother, when all other arguments had failed.

Who "Old Dead" was, Flossie had n't the least idea; but she knew he must be somebody to be dreaded, for the name alone struck terror to her gentle soul; and even Fluff, bold as he was, had often submitted to his older brothers, when they threatened to summon "Old Dead."

Thus, much against her will, Flossie yielded, and promised to help her brothers deceive their kind parents in regard to her poor lost brother; and when Squirrella and Squirrello returned, the sad story was told them that Fluff had suddenly disappeared, and that they thought the fierce Blinkeye must have carried him off.

"In the daytime?" asked Squirrello. "How can that be? He sleeps all day long."

"Any way, we heard a great noise, and thought it must be Blinkeye," asserted the little squirrels, boldly.

But in spite of their success in deceiv-

ing their parents, the cowardly little creatures were far from being satisfied with
themselves; and as for little Flossie, she
mourned more and more, as day after day
passed, and no tidings came from her
favorite brother.

Poor Fluff! he was in the power of
old Rough, who was keeping him a prisoner, in order to revenge himself on Squirrello and Squirrella for giving assistance to
Bobtilla. Ruffina was his jailor, and heard
without pity his prayers to be released.

The old miser himself occasionally visited
his captive in order to enjoy his misery.
Poor little Fluff! One who had seen him
in his days of freedom, with his bushy tail
tilted saucily over his striped back, and
his bright eyes glancing roguishly about,
would never recognize him in the drooping
little figure with lustreless eyes that now
crouched in one corner of old Rough's prison,
day and night under Ruffina's sharp eyes, as

she sat ready to pounce upon him at the first effort he made to escape.

Very meagre was poor Fluff's fare, and the plump sides that once bulged out under his generous feed of nuts were now sunken and hollow.

At first the little prisoner, relying on his swift movements, made many attempts to escape when he thought the attention of his watchful jailor was withdrawn; but he was soon undeceived, and her strong paws reminded him that she was as vigilant as ever.

Courageous as was Fluff's spirit, it was fast becoming subdued from imprisonment and starvation; but through it all came the thought that his loving parents would find some means to release him, and this thought cheered him through many a lonely hour.

Little did Fluff dream, frank and fearless as he was, to what base methods cowardly natures can be led; and shut up in this dark cavern, his mind pictured his brothers and sister lurking near his prison, watching for an opportunity to defend him, and his parents laying plans for his release. Every sound made his heart beat fast with expectation, but each time it fell with disappointment as his hopes deceived him.

While poor Fluff waited and watched for his release, his friends outside were busily employed in discovering traces of him. In vain did Squirrello and Squirrella search for some trace of their lost child, and Bobtilla joined in the search.

That shrewd fellow, the swallow Swift, flew hither and thither, looking into hollow trees and dark holes; but not a clew to the missing Fluff did he discover.

That experienced detective, Flipwing, was on the watch, too, and at night prowled silently about, hoping to gain some clew to the whereabouts of Fluff. At times some slight information, that to the inexperienced would seem of no value, the shrewd Flipwing would seize on, and by skilfully weaving together the news he had obtained, the hope that he had at last found a clew to the mystery would encourage him; but when the chain of evidence was nearly complete, a missing link would overthrow the whole, and Flipwing's patient work become useless.

At last, however, when the detective's final hope had disappeared, an unexpected event set his heart beating with renewed courage.

"The squirrels looked as they were directed, and discovered
the bat."

CHAPTER XV.

FLIPWING MAKES AN IMPORTANT DISCOVERY.

THE circumstance that so much encouraged the bat Flipwing was the following: One morning, after an unusually

tedious night had been spent in trying to discover some information concerning the missing Fluff, Flipwing had alighted on a tree in the depths of the wood, and clinging head downward to the rough bark had fallen instantly asleep.

The sun's rays sifting through the forest-trees did not wake the exhausted bat, and he slept soundly until the sun stood directly overhead. Then his heavy slumber changed to a lighter one, interspersed with dreams in which the scenes of the previous night were enacted. At last Flipwing dreamed that his diligent search was rewarded, and the fate of the lost squirrel decided.

So vivid was the dream that Flipwing could hardly believe it was not reality, and that he did not actually hear the voice of the little squirrel, when suddenly a particularly bright ray of sunlight fell on him, and he awoke.

At first so deep had been his slumber,

and so very natural his dream, that the bat could not at once understand whether he were awake or asleep. He looked about him, however, and soon realized that he had been asleep on the tree where he had alighted a few hours before. The atmosphere of his dream hung about him, and he still seemed to hear the little squirrel's high tones.

It was true that Flipwing *did* hear a squirrel's voice; but it was not the voice of Fluff, and in an instant the bat's sharp senses were wide awake and on the alert. Three young squirrels were seated on a neighboring tree, so eager in conversation that they did not observe the small, dark outline of the bat clinging to the tree. Flossie and her two older brothers were talking together very eagerly, and after hearing a few words Flipwing did not allow a single sentence of the conversation to escape him.

"Do let me tell what became of him,"

pleaded Flossie; "he may be alive, and waiting for us to release him."

"Remember your promise, you little sneak!" answered her brother Bob; "you need n't think you can go back on that."

"Fluff would n't have served you so, you know he would n't," said Flossie, earnestly. "He 'd have come right into the hole and tried to get you out."

"Well, we 're not quite so foolish as all that," said Chippie, the other brother. "It would n't have helped Fluff any to have us caught and eaten up too."

"Oh dear!" exclaimed Flossie, "then you think poor Fluff is killed? Oh, how wicked we have been not to tell!"

"I don't believe he 's killed," replied Bob; "most likely he 's alive and well, and they 're only keeping him there in prison."

"Then there 's all the more reason for our telling," said Flossie. "Just think of his waiting for some one to come and help him, while we are such cowards we don't dare tell what happened to him!"

"If you *do* tell, Floss, 'old Dead' will get you sure, and I'll call him," threatened Bob, for Flossie was becoming so earnest that her brother felt extreme measures were needed.

"I don't care for 'old Dead'! You can call him, for all I care. I'm going to tell just where poor Fluff is," and off started Flossie with more energy than she had ever before displayed.

So unexpected was their gentle little sister's revolt that her brothers at first were too much astonished to move; but they recovered themselves before she had gone very far, and soon overtook her, handling her so roughly that the poor little creature gave a cry of pain.

"Let her alone! Do you hear?" called out a voice, sharply.

All three of the squirrels looked about

them in astonishment; but not a trace of
the speaker did they discover, and a horrible
thought began to dawn in Chippie's mind,
that perhaps " old Dead," on whose name
they had so often called, had become tired
of these appeals, and had at last come to
call them to account.

"Let her alone, I say!" repeated the
voice; "and stop where you are, or it will
be the worse for you."

Too terrified to move, the three young
squirrels waited breathlessly for the pos-
sessor of the voice to disclose himself. In
vain their eyes glanced anxiously about, —
not a sign of any living creature did they
discover.

"Look up here, on this oak-tree," called
out the same voice. "There's nothing to
be afraid of. All I want of you is to
answer a question or two, and then you
shall go."

The squirrels looked as they were directed, and discovered the bat. The discovery was a great relief to them, particularly to Chippie, whose imagination had become quite active on the subject of "old Dead."

"Now tell me where your brother is. I promise you that nobody shall harm you if you tell the truth."

The two brothers were silent, and looked at each other inquiringly, as if they were deliberating whether they should tell all they knew. The bat was very quick to see what was going on in their minds.

"If you tell me all," said Flipwing, "I will not betray you; but unless you do, I shall go at once to your parents and repeat to them the conversation I have overheard."

Thus warned, Bob recited the same story he had repeated to his parents about Fluff's sudden disappearance.

"You are not telling me the truth," said Flipwing, severely; "remember, I overheard you just now when you thought yourselves alone."

"I will tell you all about it," said Flossie, boldly. "Fluff went into a dark hole after some acorns, and he did n't come back; and he gave an awfully loud screech, and I know something must have hurt him very badly, for Fluff does n't make a fuss about trifles."

"Where is the hole into which your brother went, little one?" asked Flipwing, kindly.

"Do you see that big stump over by that tall hemlock-tree?" asked Flossie.

"I can't see very well in the day-time, little one; but if you describe it, I can find it when night comes."

"There's a big stump right over there," said Flossie, with a nod of her head in the direction indicated. "It's a *very* big stump, and you may know it by the lots of moss growing on top of it. Well, under it is a hole. You don't notice it at first, because it's almost covered over with leaves and moss, but Fluff pushed them aside, and it's very large indeed inside."

"And so Fluff disappeared inside, and that's the last you've seen of him, is it?"

"Yes," answered Flossie, "and I should not be surprised if an awfully cross creature with long claws lived there."

"We'll find out all about that, little one," said Flipwing; "but why did n't you tell all this before?"

Flossie hung down her head, and the two brothers looked heartily ashamed of themselves.

"I see how it is," said the acute Flipwing; "you wanted to tell, and your brothers would n't allow you to. Well, I promised not to betray you if you told me all; but such cowardly actions deserve to be punished, and I should think your consciences would keep you uneasy. I would n't want *my* conscience burdened with the thought that I had left a brother of mine in the lurch."

The two cowardly brothers did indeed look as if their consciences were beginning to work, for they hung their heads in a very shamefaced manner, and made no reply.

" Now you can go," said Flipwing, " for I wish to be alone to think; " and off ran the squirrels, delighted to be released. Even the two cowardly brothers were greatly relieved to know that the bat had taken it upon himself to find their lost brother.

All through the day Flipwing remained silently hanging to his tree, and when night came he suddenly unfolded his long wings and floated noiselessly away.

That same evening old Rough visited his prisoner, and found everything going on most satisfactorily. The little squirrel was as pitiful an object as even he could desire, his former animation gone, and his once plump body grown very meagre under his scanty fare. All this made the old miser particularly happy, and he emerged from his den with a repulsive grin on his grim countenance. Ruffina cautiously followed him; and as he emerged from the den, he turned and saw her behind him.

"What are you here for? Go back to your charge," said the old miser, angrily.

"Do please allow me a little more to eat;" said Ruffina, meekly; "it is so very little that I grow weaker every day, and I often have a dreadful pain inside."

"More to eat!" snarled the old rat. "Are you crazy? What do you suppose will become of us unless we are very saving? Yes, old lady, we must pinch and save, unless we wish to die of want."

"I shall die of starvation unless I have more to eat," answered Ruffina, made bold by sheer desperation. "You don't allow me enough to keep body and soul together, and I don't dare leave your prisoner there long enough to go to seek any."

"You'd better not, madam," said the old rat, with a savage snap of his teeth that caused his wife to start back. "You'd better not! I allow you all you need to keep alive. A nice state of affairs there would be if you had your own way!"

"But why not make ourselves comfortable, when you have so much stored away?" pleaded Ruffina.

A sudden spring toward her by the old miser caused Ruffina to give a terrified squeak, and rush back into the den. Her husband looked after her for a moment, and then with a leer of satisfaction he departed.

When he was out of sight, a little dark object emerged from a neighboring tree, and alighted on a bush that grew near the entrance to the den; it was Flipwing the spy, who from his place of concealment had overheard the conversation between the old miser and his wife.

"Ruffina!" called Flipwing.

The summons was repeated several times before the long, sharp nose of the wary Ruffina was seen emerging from the entrance of the den.

"Oh, there you are!" said Flipwing. "I want to have a few words with you."

When she heard her name called, Ruffina poked her long nose farther out, and cast a sharp glance about her. Nobody was in sight; and she was about to retreat when she once more heard the same voice, and following the direction of the sound discovered the little bat.

Now Ruffina was very timid and submissive in the presence of her lord and master, but when out of his presence was as bold as anybody; and so she answered gruffly,—

"What do you want at this time of night?"

"I want a little talk with you," answered Flipwing.

"Well, talk away," said Ruffina.

It was not easy for Flipwing to begin, for having seen Ruffina so timid with her husband, he was quite unprepared for this change of manner.

"I say, it's a shame the old man is so hard on you," began Flipwing, after a moment's pause.

"What's that to you, pray?" asked Ruffina, shortly.

"I don't like to see it," replied Flipwing, determined not to be bluffed by this cool reception. "The old fellow ought to be more considerate of you; there are plenty of younger fellows who would gladly stand in his shoes."

"Nonsense!" responded Ruffina, bruskly, but in a tone that showed she was not displeased with this broad flattery.

"Fact," said Flipwing, "and you know it!"

"I don't know any such thing," replied Ruffina.

"You 'll not make me believe that," said Flipwing. "Did n't you ever see yourself reflected in a brook or pool?"

"Well, suppose I have, — what then?"

Flipwing was rather discomfited to find he had made so little headway in the good graces of the miser's wife; he had imagined that a little flattery would make a favorable impression.

"I was going to say," remarked the bat, "that it is a pity old Rough keeps you so short, for a little more food would make your coat shine till you could see your face in it, — not but that it is handsome as it is, but better fare would make it more so."

"Well, what of it?" asked Ruffina.

"I was about to add that I could show you where you could eat to your heart's content, and take away all you could carry besides. It is but a short distance from here."

"No, you don't!" exclaimed Ruffina, with a shrewd grin.

"What do you mean?" asked Flipwing, innocently.

"I mean, what do you expect me to do in return?"

"Why, nothing," answered the bat; "can't you give me credit for being a little disinterested? I hear you complaining to your husband that you have not enough to eat, and he harshly refuses to grant you a larger allowance; what more natural than that I should tell you where you can find what you want? It does n't cost me any-thing, — *I* don't eat acorns."

"Acorns!" exclaimed Ruffina, her mouth fairly watering at the mention of the rich, juicy nuts. "Well, where are they?"

"Do you know the two big chestnut-trees in Farmer Smith's pasture? The lightning struck one of them last summer and split it. Well, under that one you will find a hole with some large acorns in it. I saw some squirrels hiding them there. You just go and help yourself."

"I can't!" answered Ruffina. "Rough would kill me if he knew I left the den."

"He will not know anything about it," said Flipwing.

"He knows everything," replied Ruffina; "and then I could n't leave —" She stopped abruptly, for in her eagerness for the food for which she was suffering she had nearly allowed the secret of the prison to escape her.

"Well, no matter," replied Flipwing, "do as you like about it; the nuts are there and will keep."

"It 's of no use," said Ruffina, decidedly; "Rough would be sure to come home the very moment I had left, and then —" A shiver which was more expressive than words ran through her emaciated frame.

"I 'm sorry," replied the bat, good-naturedly, "for I don't know when I 've seen such fine specimens; they were evidently picked expressly."

"It 's very kind of you to tell me about them," said Ruffina, "but it is impossible for me to go so far;" and with a shake of her head she slowly re-entered the den.

"She 'll go," said Flipwing to himself, "and before long too. The poor creature is nearly starved to death, and can't resist the temptation. Well, I will watch my chance, and rescue poor Fluff, if he does not die of grief and starvation before;" and away flew Flipwing, well satisfied with the result of his expedition.

"And then swam quietly home."

CHAPTER XVI.

OLD ROUGH EXPOUNDS A LAW OF THE WOODS,
AND OLD CAW FORMS A PLAN.

AFTER old Rough had left his little prisoner, instead of going in the direction
of his home he entered deeper into the
woods. There was no moon, and the stars
were obscured by dark clouds that drifted
rapidly across the sky, while a stiff breeze
swayed the tree-tops until they jostled one

another roughly, and groaned and creaked. Occasionally a low muttering that resounded through the forest and died away in a faint wail was heard from the dark clouds overhead.

All the small inhabitants of the woods, with the exception of a solitary bat that crossed and recrossed old Rough's path, were safe within their snug homes, and the old water-rat went on through the darkness with more confidence than if the way were lighted for him. Occasionally he stopped and sniffed about with his long, sharp nose; but it was evident that important business was afoot, for he proceeded with as much haste as his bulky body and the uneven forest roads permitted.

Darker grew the clouds, and more violently the tree-tops crashed against one another, while the heavy rolls of thunder seemed to shake the earth.

The louder, however, the thunder growled, and the denser the darkness, the better pleased was old Rough as he scurried along among the underbrush, unmoved by the commotion about him. After a time he stopped and gazed at the tall trees.

"It should be near here," remarked the old rat to himself. "I am sure he said the big oak in front of the ledge of rocks. He'll be sure to be at home on such a night as this, so I shall not have had my journey for nothing. Yes, there's the ledge, and the big oak too; and unless I'm much mistaken, there's the old fellow himself on the lookout as usual. He's a fine looking fellow, is Blinkeye, that's a fact; but I prefer to keep at a safe distance."

About half way up the old oak, where once a sturdy limb had been torn away by the lightning, the wood had become decayed and crumbled, and in the natural hollow thus formed, the owl had made his nest. There he sat, protected from the weather, the pointed tufts on his head erect, and his vigilant yellow eyes on the watch for any prey that might fall to him.

As the water-rat neared the oak-tree, the slight rustling he made as he dragged his body over the leaves and grass was detected by the quick ears of the watchful owl.

"A bad night to be out in, friend Rough," observed the owl, as the rat paused under the oak-tree.

"I don't find it so," answered Rough. "I prefer having the road to myself; and a little rain would suit me to a T."

There was a short pause, during which the branches crashed fiercely together, and a loud report from the black clouds reverberated through the dark forest, and in the momentary silence that followed this explosion of the elements was heard the pattering of large rain-drops. Faster and faster came the drops, and soon down came the rain in sheets.

The owl drew farther within his retreat,

and sat with his wings drawn closely to his sides, and his head held stiffly back, to avoid the drops that at times splashed against him. Not so the water-rat; exposed to the full force of the shower, in a few moments his heavy fur was drenched; but an expression of enjoyment stole over his countenance as the rain ran in little rivers down his sides, and trickled off his long nose.

"I suppose you strolled out to enjoy this fine evening," said Blinkeye, with a shrug of his shoulders, as a shower of raindrops dashed against his face.

"No," answered the water-rat, frankly, "I came to see you on business."

"I'm at your service," replied Blinkeye.

"You know, of course, how that Italian fellow Trillo turned out?" said Rough.

"Yes, I have heard he disappeared, after he had made use of his friends. It is just as I expected it would be."

"It served them right for being such toadies," sneered the water-rat. "That cracked Katy Did (for that's her real name, though she doesn't consider it fine enough since she's made poetry) I'm told sat up nights making verses about him. I'm glad he went off without paying his debts, to teach them a lesson."

"Teach them a lesson!" repeated Blink-eye, with a cynical laugh.

"You're right," said the old miser, with an approving nod; "I see you understand animal nature. But I must come to business, for it's getting late and I am some distance from home. You know the war between the frogs and mice that's to take place,—. you must have heard it talked over."

"Yes," replied Blinkeye; "and if it's ever to come off, I should say it was time to begin."

"It *will* begin at once now. Since Johnny the basso was so put out by Trillo leaving him in the lurch, he's turned his attention to the war."

"What is he up to?" asked the owl.

"He's putting things into shape. He's been canvassing all the bogs about, and they say he's got a big army together. He's smart, is Johnny, and I wouldn't give much for the mice's chances."

"Think not?" asked Blinkeye.

"No, sir," replied old Rough, confidently. "Why, the frogs are ten to one of them; and a fine set of fellows they are, I can tell you. I've seen them drilling nights down by our bog. No, indeed, the mice haven't a shadow of a chance."

"Frogs are not to my taste, but sleek, tender young mice —" said Blinkeye, with a snap of his strong beak that was very expressive.

"That's just it," said old Rough, eagerly. "It's for your interest and mine to have Johnny's army win, and I've promised to help him all I can (in the way of advice, you know); and if I find an opportunity to do the mice an ill turn, I shall take advantage of it, you may be sure."

"I don't see exactly how it is for your and my interest to have the frogs victorious," said Blinkeye.

"Don't you see? Why, the mice will be obliged to retreat in confusion, and you will have a chance to take your pick of them."

"Oh, yes, I understand," replied the owl, who in spite of his wise expression and reputation for wisdom was not nearly so acute as the old water-rat. "And you, what will you gain?"

"I? Oh, I shall look in on their homes while they're fighting, and help myself, you may be sure, to the stores I find there. The mice, as a general thing, are thrifty and saving; but the frogs are shiftless fellows, and live from hand to mouth."

"When is the battle to take place?" asked Blinkeye.

"I don't know exactly," replied the water-rat; "but as soon as Johnny is ready. By the way, what is that law of the woods I've heard you repeat?"

"You mean that prophecy my great-grandfather recited when the crow and your great-grandfather —"

"Yes," interrupted the rat, hastily, "what is it?"

The owl gravely recited, —

> "'War and strife, grief and woe,
> Follow you where'er you go.
> Never more shall you know rest
> For weary feet and aching breast,
> Till body round and lithe and long
> Shall vanquish body thick and strong.
> Then shall dawn a day of peace,
> And every strife and sorrow cease.'

Is that what you meant?" he added.

"Yes," replied old Rough, "that's it. It evidently refers to the battle that's to come off between the frogs and the mice. Yes, 'body round and lithe and long' must refer to the frogs, for they can lengthen out to any extent, and 'body thick and strong' of course means the mice, though I don't know about the strength. Yes, there's no doubt but that 'body round and lithe and long' *will* 'vanquish body thick and strong.'"

"I presume," said Blinkeye, "the mice are preparing too?"

"By no means," replied old Rough. "I don't believe they have the least notion of what a battle is, — they are timid creatures."

"I know it, afraid of their own shadows," said Blinkeye, as a sudden streak of lightning flashed in his face, and made him flutter his wings nervously.

"They keep out of the way so much that they don't know what is going on in the world," said the water-rat. "Oh, 't will be an easy victory for the frogs! Whew! what was that?" he exclaimed, as a dark object rushed by him and nearly brushed against his nose.

"Only a bat; the woods are full of them. They're not worth the trouble of catching, they're all wings," replied the owl, coolly.

"One passed me on the way here," said the old rat; "I should n't be surprised if it were the same one. Well, I must be off. Keep a sharp lookout for the engagement, for it may take place any night now."

The owl retreated farther into his den, and the old rat retraced his steps, slipping along on the wet ground with great ease, until he came to his native stream, when he plunged in, and disappearing under the turbid water, arose some distance farther on, and then swam quietly home, his long nose only visible, as it parted the surface of the stream, forming ripples that spread to either bank.

The dark object that flew so near the old water-rat, as he was conversing with the owl, was, as the latter had said, a bat, and no other than our sharp friend Flipwing, who had followed the old miser to the owl's abode, and had overheard the conversation between the two. Long before the old water-rat reached his den, the general of the mouse forces, a brother-in-law of Bobtilla, and General Squeako by name, was apprised of all that was going on among the frogs; and a long consultation was held between him and the bat, which seemed to be satisfactory to both parties. Shortly before daylight, Flipwing reached his home, wet and tired, and instantly fell asleep.

Not so the mouse-general. Sleep did not visit his eyes that night; but under cover of the darkness he made the rounds of his soldiers, trusting to no one but himself, to make sure that all was in readiness.

The next morning old Caw awoke even earlier than was his usual habit, for the heavy showers of the night before were followed by a particularly fresh and invigorating atmosphere. The refreshed foliage glistened and quivered as the light breeze stirred it, and the rays of the sun caused the dew-drops on the grass to sparkle like crystals.

Every bird felt the influence of the freshness that pervaded Nature, and their morning songs rang out more blithely, until the forest was alive with the sweet melody.

Old Caw stretched himself, and then hopped down to the bough beneath him. The other members of the crow family were just beginning to stir, and were cawing sleepily to one another.

"The early bird catches the worm," said old Caw to himself, as he noiselessly spread his wings and flew away.

The old crow reaped a fine harvest this morning, for driven to the surface by the heavy rain, many an earth-worm was seized by Caw's strong beak before he could wriggle back to his hole. Grubs, too, reposing unsuspecting of evil on the wet earth, were snapped up by the voracious Caw.

The shrewd old crow discovered before long that something of unusual importance was about to take place, for the field-mice, who were usually safe at home at that hour, were hurrying about, talking together in low tones, all conversation ceasing and groups dispersing as soon as he made his appearance. All this excited old Caw's curiosity, and determined him to fathom the mystery.

In the course of his morning's wanderings, old Caw alighted to rest near the stump beneath which poor little Fluff was concealed. As he sat pluming his ruffled feathers, that in his old age required more care than in his youth when they were glossy and flexible, low tones fell on his ear; and in an instant the old crow's head was turned to one side, with his best ear tilted toward the opening beneath the stump, whence the voices proceeded.

Old Caw was not long in recognizing the voice of old Rough, and, in her occasional submissive replies, the high, squeaking one of Ruffina; and judging from his low tones that the old miser was desirous that the conversation should not be overheard, Caw approached as near as he dared without fear of detection, and listened with all his might.

"When, did you say?" squeaked Ruffina.

"I did n't say when," replied her husband, in the snarling tone in which he habitually addressed his wife. "Whenever the frogs are ready; so all you have to do is to hold yourself in readiness, and do as I tell you."

"But how shall I know when the battle

has begun? I can't hear anything in this lonely place."

"I shall let you know," replied her husband; "and mind you follow my directions implicitly. You are certain you understand just what is expected of you, and will not spoil all by your stupidity?"

"Yes," replied Ruffina, meekly; "I'm to visit all the mouse-nests while the fight is going on, and bring away whatever I find there."

"Don't speak so loudly; you've got a voice like a trumpet," answered her husband, sharply; "and mind you don't waste your time among the poor ones, but go at once to the rich mice, who have piles of grain stored away;" and the old rat's small black eyes snapped with pleasure at the prospect, while his wife, poor hungry creature, felt her heart leap within her.

"Remember you are not to taste of one single grain or kernel, or it will be the dearest morsel you ever ate," added the old miser, savagely.

"Yes, Rough," answered his submissive wife.

"I've heard all I want to know," said old Caw to himself, as he silently flew away that he might not be detected by the two rats. He left the woods, and flew directly to the farm where old Rough, a short time before, had fought so desperately with the weasel.

The old crow perched on an apple-tree that grew near the barnyard, and kept his one eye roaming about in every direction. The hens were busily engaged in eating their breakfast, for the inhabitants of a farm begin the day early. The horses in their stalls were munching their feed, while in the barnyard the cows stood placidly chewing their cuds during the process of milking.

Of all these things old Caw took note, as

he sat on the apple-tree, hidden by the foliage, and careful not to attract the attention of any of the farm-hands by the least motion; for nobody knew better than he the unpopularity of his race among farmers. He waited until the milkers had carried to the farm-house their pails of white, foaming milk, and then, after a careful survey of the premises, to make sure that nobody was in sight, he silently flew down from his hiding-place, and walking up to the hole that he knew led to the weasel's abode, softly called his name.

In a few moments the head of the weasel appeared, and an earnest conversation ensued between the two. So low were the voices of both pitched that not a word could have been audible to any listener; but the result of the interview was evidently highly satisfactory, for the weasel looked very happy, and the old crow flew home, cawing exultingly.

"The hitherto orderly retreat of the frogs was turned into an
ignominious stampede."

CHAPTER XVII.

THE BATTLE.

IT was a warm, sultry night in August;
the air was heavy with vapor, and the
grass wet with dew. The large meadow
through which the stream ran was seen
through a haze from the clouds of vapor
that settled down over it, and which the

still air had not power to lift. Through
this mist the outline of the forest that
surrounded the meadow was dimly seen, the
tall trees looking gaunt and ghostlike in
the faint light.

The large bog that was formed by the
widening of the stream was hardly visible
from the dense mist that stood over it, and
as the great red moon sank behind the forest-trees, darkness settled down over all,
until the meadow looked ghostly white, enveloped in its veil of mist.

A little knoll rose on one side of the
meadow, and when the moon disappeared,
and all was dark and still, little lights were
seen flitting to and fro. Presently the
mist on the meadow seemed to be broken
by innumerable little dark objects that
emerged from the edge of the bog, inter-
mingled with numerous lights gleaming here
and there through the vapor. Gradually
these lines lengthened out into lines par-

allel with one another, and spread out on each side of the bog, the same little lights scintillating among them and lighting them on their way.

Soon the same little sparks might have been seen darting down from the knoll, and running thence in various directions toward the lines forming in the meadow by the bog. The little knoll served as the headquarters of the frog-general, who sent out his aids-de-camp, the fireflies, with orders for his divisions of valiant soldiers who were issuing from the bog, armed with sharp spears of grass, wherewith to attack the wily enemy.

Gradually the dark lines spread out in a semicircle across the meadow, brilliantly illuminated from time to time by the glinting of the fireflies, who at intervals, as if by command, emitted brilliant light, while answering signals flashed from the reeds in the bog to show that the reserves were holding themselves in readiness.

As the general on the knoll directs his gaze toward the opposite wood, he beholds tiny blue lights, their steady glow contrasting with the scintillating lights of his fire-flies, — the steady glow rising and falling and moving among the grass where the meadow merges from the wood.

The frog-general finds his expectations verified; his preparations, though secretly and carefully undertaken, have been discovered by the enemy, the field-mice, under command of that able soldier, General Squeako. He had pressed the glow-worms into his service, and they were aiding him by their steady, phosphorescent light.

Regiment after regiment of well-drilled field-mice does the frog-general see mustering for the fray, silently taking their positions, endeavoring to extend their flank, lengthening out their lines, which he fears will overlap his own.

Fearing that his forces will be outflanked, like the cunning tactician that he is, the frog-general determines on a ruse. Accordingly he gives the order to his most valiant regiment to advance a company of soldiers, accompanied by torch-bearers, beyond the extreme left wing of the enemy, in order to make General Squeako think that there is to be the attack.

The mouse-general, however, being aware of his old friend Johnny's wily tricks, understands that this is only a ruse, and determining to frustrate the attempt, immediately issues the order, —

"Glow-worms, shut lanterns, and columns advance upon the enemy under cover of darkness."

The order is obeyed with military promptness, and not a mouse in the ranks quails. At the same time his pickets return, confirming the mouse-general's opinion that the brilliancy and hubbub raised by the frogs on the left wing is only a harmless band of fireflies and a company of soldiers, and not an attacking division supported by soldiers.

In the mean time the pickets of the advancing mouse-columns hit upon those of the frogs, who, being brilliantly illuminated, afford the mice an opportunity to make an attack — which under cover of darkness on their side is accomplished with great energy and dash — upon the centre of the unsuspecting frog-army.

The battle, now beginning in the centre, rages in earnest, — mouse grapples frog, and frog grapples mouse in deadly contest; biting and wrestling, kicking and scratching, the valiant combatants mingle in terrible groups.

The orderly lines are broken; the agonized squeaking of the mice, and the dying "a-hungs" of the frogs, make night hideous. Both generals urge on their forces from either wing, and the carnage becomes universal. The orderly lines of fireflies change into disorderly clouds of sparks; while the rear columns of the mice, taking advantage of the confusion, advance to the battle-field, lighted by orderly bands of steady glow-worms, driving back stragglers and deserters, to strengthen the lines in front.

For a time the fortunes of war tremble in the balance. The frogs, forced to give way, are driven by the valiant mice to the edge of the bog, and the more timid ones in the rear, thinking the battle lost, spring into the water; but at that moment a deep-booming " a-hung!" is heard amid the bull-rushes, where the valiant frog-general has removed his staff; a million of lights illumine the swamp, and lo! as if by magic, the reserves are seen issuing from the bog, swimming toward the shore, and reinforcing the yielding lines. They repulse by renewed attack the mouse-centre, through which they threaten to break.

It was the water-rat who had by his advice aided the frog-reserves; and during the engagement the shrewd old fellow had squatted behind the bog, and taken in every movement of both parties. Confident that owing to the secrecy employed by the frogs the field-mice would be taken unawares and unprepared, great was his astonishment to find General Squeako's division so well organized and generalled. Not a little uneasiness did he feel, as the contest progressed, and the field-mice forced the frog-army back to the bog.

The mouse-forces also had their reserves waiting for the word of command to advance; and the word was given at the proper moment by the astute Squeako, the columns moving in double-quick time to the edge of the bog, where the battle was raging indecisively. The hitherto orderly retreat of the frogs was turned into an ignominious stampede. Leaping and plunging into the bog by thousands, the water fairly foamed. Those in the rear, in their frantic efforts to reach the water's edge, jumped upon the struggling mass in front, crushing many, and tumbling them about in confusion. All those who were not incapacitated, safely dived into the water out of reach of the mice, who stood squeaking with joy and exultation on the edge of the bog.

Thus ended the great battle between the mice and the frogs. Those of the frogs that remained alive having escaped in safety, General Squeako ordered a retreat, and dismissed his troops at the edge of the wood.

While this terrible battle was raging, Ruffina, being apprised by her husband that the frogs were in readiness to move on the enemy, made her preparations accordingly.

With great anxiety she waited until the decisive hour arrived, bustling about nervously meanwhile inside her den, and making frequent excursions to the entrance, where she turned her sharp eyes anxiously on the large red moon that was slowly settling down to the tops of the forest trees. As soon as the last spot of red disappeared, and the woods were enveloped in darkness, after carefully inspecting little Fluff, who lay curled up in his corner fast asleep, and making sure that his slumber was deep, Ruffina issued cautiously forth.

The sharp-witted little bat Flipwing you may be sure was aware of everything that took place in the neighborhood of the little prisoner, whom he had pledged himself to rescue. From his hiding-place near by he saw the old miser's wife depart, and, watching her movements until she disappeared into the woods, he at once flew down to the entrance of the old rat's den, and putting his head inside the opening, gently called the squirrel's name.

Poor little Fluff, weakened by grief and hardships, was sleeping soundly, and dreaming of the happy home that was once his.' In his dreams he was again at play with his brothers and sister, frisking over the tall trees, and jumping from bough to bough. It was no wonder that when he heard his name called, he considered it as a part of his dream, for Flipwing's pleasant voice was a striking contrast to Ruffina's shrill, scolding tones, and the miser's harsh voice. So little Fluff slept on until the call was repeated several times.

Gradually the little prisoner awoke to the reality that he was in the old rat's den, and that a voice very unlike Ruffina's or her husband's was calling him.

"Fluff, wake up!" he now distinctly heard; and starting to his feet, he was wide awake in an instant.

"Who calls me?" asked the little squirrel, timidly, for the voice was a new one, and the hope he had at first entertained of friends coming to his relief had long since deserted him.

"No matter who I am; you don't know me, but I come from your friends. Ruffina is away, and if you are ever to escape, now is the time. So hurry and come out."

Fluff looked anxiously toward the place where Ruffina usually slept, and it was indeed empty. So severe, however, had been the little prisoner's experiences since his capture, that he had lost faith in everybody; and now how could he tell but that this was a ruse of Ruffina to try him? And if he were retaken, what frightful consequences would ensue!

Thus reasoned Fluff; and meanwhile the stranger outside was entreating him to come out.

"You will never have another such

chance," urged the voice, "and our time is short; so make haste, if you value your freedom."

Although reduced to a condition of misery and despair by his imprisonment, as Fluff heard these words some of his old energy returned to him.

"Nothing can be worse than my present condition," reasoned the poor little squirrel, "and now that I have the chance offered me, I will take it;" and he crawled to the opening of the den. Although he had never seen the little bat before, after one look at his honest face he unhesitatingly followed him.

The fresh air, of which he had been so long deprived, infused hope and courage into the little captive's heart, and he exerted himself to the utmost to keep pace with his guide; but so cramped had been the quarters in the den that the legs once so strong and active were now weak and tremulous, and progress was slow and uncertain. How different was it from the bounds and leaps Fluff made when in imagination he found himself once more free!

"Have patience, and we 'll soon be there," said Flipwing, kindly, as he noticed the squirrel's efforts. "We are safe now, — all the water-rats in the world could n't get you; but let me advise you not to venture so far from home in future."

"You may be sure of that," replied Fluff, decidedly; "once let me reach home, that 's all!"

Now familiar landmarks began to present themselves to the little squirrel, — trees over which he had run, and stumps beneath which he had hidden; and his tired feet grew lighter at the sight.

There it was at last, the dear old tree, beneath which was the warm nest he never expected to see again; and giving a loud chirrup of joy, in sprang the lost Fluff, and in an instant was nestling against his mother's soft breast.

To return to Ruffina. As has been stated, she left the den, and entered the forest. The darkness that followed the setting of the moon was just what she desired for her expedition, and she chuckled to herself as she proceeded.

The families of the mice-soldiers had all repaired to the edge of the wood, that they might watch the contest going on in the meadow, and their homes were deserted. This, however, made little difference to Ruffina, for the large water-rat was more than a match for a whole family of little field-mice.

How Ruffina's eyes glistened, as in the first home she entered, her eyes fell on stores of grain laid by for the next winter's use!

"First of all, I'll fill myself just as full as I can," said Ruffina, "for Rough will not

give me anything of what I bring home, —
he 'll keep it all to trade with;" and the
half-famished creature helped herself to the
rich food before her until she had made a
heartier meal than had fallen to her lot
since she united her fortunes to those of
the old miser.

When she could eat no more, Ruffina
stopped, and was startled to find how little
remained of the former piles of grain.

"No matter," said the water-rat to herself; "there are many more places as good
as this, and now that I 've had a good
supper I can work all the faster. I 'll go
next to Squeako's, — they say he 's got more
stored away than all the rest put together.
I must n't forget, though, to do as Rough
told me;" and she tore apart with her
strong paws the carefully made beds, scat-
tering the contents about.

Very near was the den where the mouse-
general lived, and that, too, was deserted.

Quite grand and spacious were the long passageways leading to the main dwelling-room. Ruffina was familiar with the plan adopted by both rats and mice in the construction of their dwellings, and the home of the wealthy General Squeako did not differ from the rest, except that the passageways diverging from the main entrance were more spacious and numerous than in the homes of the poorer mice.

Ruffina entered one of these passages, and proceeded at once to the interior of the den. Very large and high was this room; and the water-rat's sharp eyes at once detected piles of grain recently stored, and scraps of meat and pork so tempting, that in spite of her recent hearty repast, she could not resist the temptation of nibbling. She knew, however, that her time was short; so she began at once to carry out the stores and deposit them in a place of safety, until the old miser should find time to remove them.

While busily engaged in her work, Ruffina heard a slight rustling at the entrance of the cave. This did not disturb her, however, for she knew she was more than a match for the mouse-general himself, so she carelessly turned her head in the direction of the sound.

In an instant Ruffina's whole manner changed, and a violent trembling seized her. The new-comer was no timid mouse; the wary water-rat knew, before his head appeared, that the deadliest enemy of her tribe, the weasel, was before her.

Completely paralyzed with fear, Ruffina stood as if in a nightmare, her shaking limbs rooted to the ground, as her pursuer came wriggling silently toward her. As if bound by a spell did the old rat stand, her eyes riveted on the long, flexible body and pitiless eyes of her enemy, — without power to stir, until he approached near enough to give the final spring. Then, and not till then, did the terrified water-rat give vent to a squeal of terror, and with a gigantic effort, leap toward the opening of the cavern.

Directly behind the old water-rat was the weasel. She felt his presence, although she dared not look behind, and she knew his steady progress would enable him to keep pace with, or perhaps overreach, her nervous leaps. Once outside the cave, she stopped but for a second, to observe the situation, and then, true to the instinct of self-preservation implanted in every one of God's creatures, she started for her native element, the stream!

Thanks to the hearty meal she had just eaten, Ruffina was enabled to make a great effort. Through the white mist that enveloped the meadow, the irregularly gleaming sparks of the fireflies and the steady lights of the glow-worms, that she descried in the neighborhood of the bog, convinced her that the battle was raging in that quarter; and as she came nearer, the squeaks of wounded field-mice, and mournful "a-hungs" of disabled frogs, fell on her ears. All at once a loud hoot was heard, and she beheld the fierce Blinkeye hovering over the battle-field, watching for an opportunity to seize his prey.

With the weasel in the rear and Blinkeye above, Ruffina felt her chances of escape lessening; and driven to desperation, she gathered together all her strength, and with a few prodigious leaps gained the stream, into which she sprang, and was hidden from view beneath its protecting waters.

"As the officer spoke, the Widow O'Warty, who had been sitting
erect, gave a loud croak, and rolled once more upon her back."

CHAPTER XVIII.

THE CHAPERON.

WHILE the battle was tumultuously
raging, besides old Rough the miser
there was another interested spectator, a
very humble and timid one, — the little
brown frog Brownella. Since the faithless
tenor had departed, her life had been a

lonely one, for she was deserted by her former friends, who so short a time before had professed such admiration for the distinguished foreigner; and worse than all, her former admirer, Johnny the basso, treated her with marked indifference.

In vain did Brownella sing her most melodious songs until her voice was hoarse, and use all her arts to please the recreant basso; but the admiration she once scorned was not to be regained at will, and her former friend treated her advances with stony indifference.

With the perverseness which is said by some to characterize her sex, what she had once despised, now that it was not to be had, became very desirable, and Brownella determined to win back the affections she had lost.

Very imposing and grand was the military appearance of General Johnny, as he prepared for the coming battle; and as Brownella watched the frog-forces gathering in the meadow on the eventful night, such a longing to witness the conflict seized her, that she resolved to follow them and secrete herself where she could overlook the battle-field, and indulge in a stolen view of the valiant frog-general.

Speeding toward the place of rendezvous, the little brown frog, passing the abode of the Widow O'Warty, found that personage seated, as was her custom, in her doorway, and watching with great interest the frog-soldiers hurrying by.

"And phere is it yourself is afther going?" asked the good-natured widow, as the little brown frog was passing.

"For a little stroll this fine warm night," answered Brownella, evasively.

"It's a sthroll in the direction av the bog, I suspicion," replied the widow, slyly, "to view the military."

"Well, and what if it is?" asked Brownella. "I don't know as there is any law to prevent me from going there if I like."

"It's the law of dacency that should prevint ye," answered the widow, in a reproving tone. "The scane of war an' bloodshed is not intinded for a young cratur like yourself. It's bould an' forward ye would be accounted."

"Oh, bother!" replied Brownella, impatiently; "who cares what it's accounted! I'm going, and that settles the matter;" and off she started once more.

"Sthop!" cried the widow. "It's meself that cannot see a young cratur laying herself open to cinsure in this way. Is it a stidy, sinsible fri'nd ye possess, who would be willing to accompany ye?"

The little brown frog reflected a moment. After all it would be pleasanter to have a friend with her; and who so desirable a chaperon as the good-natured widow, who would wish to see whatever was going on?

So she replied that if the Widow O'Warty would go with her in that capacity, it would be very satisfactory.

"Sich was not me intintion," replied the widow. "Bloodshid and war have no charms for meself; but since it's detarmined to go ye are, I conc'ave it me juty to accompany ye, an' it's willin' to make a sacrifice I am;" and casting a glance about to see that all was right in her home, the chaperon hopped willingly away with her young charge.

In fact, the widow was not making the sacrifice she pretended, but was secretly glad of an excuse to witness the battle, about which her curiosity was greatly excited.

In due time the two friends arrived on the scene of action, the widow somewhat out of breath and heated, but otherwise in good condition; and the pair chose a position midway between the knoll which was the headquarters of the frog-general and the bog where he had stationed his reinforcements.

With her little heart beating with pride and affection, Brownella watched the martial figure on the knoll giving his orders to his aids-de-camp, the fireflies; and she followed them with her eyes as the shining sparks flew back and forth on their commissions. Quite excited too did the widow become, as her eyes roamed about in all directions.

Then came the mouse party, moving silently in a solid phalanx from the outskirts of the wood, the steady lights of the glow-worms scintillating among the tall meadow grass and lighting up the dusky forms of the mouse-soldiers.

" He 's a foine gineral, is Squeako, an' it 's an iligant appearance they presint," exclaimed the widow, enthusiastically.

" They are not half so nice as *our* soldiers," replied Brownella, warmly, — "great brown awkward things, with those tiresome glow-worms. Our fireflies are ever so much finer, flashing about like so many diamonds. The horrid things won't stand a shadow of a chance against our well-trained soldiers."

"Me sympathies are wid the frog-forces; but me judgemint tells me that the throops of Gineral Squeako are will conducted, an' we'll know whin the ind comes which side is the sthrongest," replied the widow, majestically.

"We shall know long before then," replied Brownella, impetuously. "Oh, the horrid, creeping things! how disgusting they are!"

In their eagerness not to lose sight of any of the events happening about them, the two spectators pressed eagerly forward, forgetting in their excitement the dangers attending a battle-field; and when the conflict was at its height, their prudence completely forsook them; and as the dying groans of the wounded fell on their ears, they pressed still nearer, to ascertain if any friends were among the slain or wounded.

At this moment, on came the frog-reinforcements from the bog, steadily and surely, like the well disciplined soldiers they were, right toward the spot where the little brown frog and her chaperon were anxiously scanning the features of the wounded heroes; when, all at once, came the order to charge, and on went the valiant frog-soldiers, their blood coursing hotly through their veins with the warlike spirit that was within them, and ferocity gleaming from every feature.

Not until late did Brownella and her chaperon perceive the solid force bearing down upon them; and Brownella, aided by her youth and agility, in a few dexterous leaps gained a place of safety, as the troops swept by.

Not so the chaperon. Too late did she become aware of the danger that threatened her, and seeing the ferocious expression of the thousands of eyes coming toward her, her presence of mind completely deserted her, and she sank on the spot, transfixed with terror. She opened her mouth to give vent to the pent-up anguish of her soul, but no sound escaped her; and even before the phalanx was upon her, the terrified chaperon rolled helplessly upon her back, where she lay convulsively kicking, while the feet of the charging soldiers passed over her ample form.

When the troops had passed, Brownella looked anxiously about for her missing chaperon, and soon discovered her lying on her back, the convulsive motions of her legs alone showing that life remained to her.

"Speak to me, dear Widow O'Warty," cried Brownella, distractedly. "Tell me you are not injured!"

Renewed convulsions on the widow's part was the only answer.

Placing her forepaws under the stout body of her chaperon, Brownella with great effort managed to roll her upon one side, where she lay kicking; but the widow was heavy and Brownella was slender, and with no amount of pushing could the little brown frog roll the solid mass any farther. The instant Brownella, from sheer exhaustion, removed the support of her slender paws, the chaperon rolled once more upon her broad back, where she lay convulsed as before.

"It's all my fault! she came here against her will to please me," groaned Brownella, with great self-reproach. "Oh, never in the world shall I forgive myself! Do speak, dearest Widow O'Warty, if only to reproach me with my thoughtlessness!"

"It's kilt entirely I am!" moaned the widow, faintly. "Oh, me poor bones!"

"Where are you injured?" asked the distressed Brownella. "In what place do you feel the most pain?"

"It's crushed fiom the crown of me h'id to the sowls of me f'ate I am," groaned the widow, as she struggled to a sitting posture; "niver agin shall I be the cratur I was afore!"

"What's the matter?" croaked a voice from behind, and an officer of the frog-army appeared.

As the officer spoke, the Widow O'Warty, who had been sitting erect, gave a loud croak, and rolled once more over upon her back, the convulsions returning with renewed energy.

"She's dead, and I've killed her!" shrieked the weeping Brownella.

"Oh, if it was something to soostain me I had, if 't was only a dhrop of wather!" moaned the widow.

"Is this the old toad we ran over just now?" asked the soldier.

"Yes, and you 've killed her!" answered Brownella, distractedly.

"Don't you believe it," said the soldier, cheerfully. "She is n't hurt; she 's overcome by fright, that 's all."

"*Fright* is it?" exclaimed the widow, suddenly reviving and assuming a sitting posture. "Fright is it ye mane? Indade, an' it 's a foine way to be talking to a body that 's kilt;" and her large eyes glared at the audacious new-comer with indignation.

"Oh, come, come, old lady, you 're not killed, that 's evident; but perhaps you are a little stunned."

"Auld lady! stunned!" repeated the widow, hysterically. "It 's not so auld I am but that I know an auld fool whin I see him."

The valiant officer, who had been through many a battle without flinching, quailed before the indignant countenance of the exasperated widow, and without casting a glance behind him, turned and actually fled!

As for the widow, her wounded pride tended to infuse energy into her listless frame; and under its reviving influence, she forgot her injuries, and betook herself homeward, giving expression at intervals to her indignation.

We will return to Ruffina, whom we left concealed from her enemy by the dark waters of her native stream. On she swam, until she reached a spot parallel with the den in which she had left her charge, little Fluff. Casting searching glances about her, to discover if her pursuer were in sight, and satisfying herself that all was safe, she left the water, and approached her abode.

Entering the den, the old water-rat looked about her, to assure herself that all was right; but the corner in which the little squirrel's form usually lay at night was empty. Ruffina passed a paw over her eyes to clear her vision, and looked again. No, she was not mistaken, the corner was indeed empty.

With feverish haste Ruffina tore apart the dried leaves that had formed little Fluff's bed, as if she expected to find concealed beneath them him whom she sought. In vain was her search, for at that very moment little Fluff was curled up by his mother's side, fast asleep.

Not a nook or cranny did Ruffina fail to search, and at last gave up the attempt as useless. Emerging from the den, she stationed herself before the entrance, and gazed frantically around her for some trace of the missing Fluff; but not a sign of him did she discern. Almost crazed at the thought of the swift vengeance that would follow the old miser's knowledge of the defeat of his plans for robbing the mice, and the disappearance of his prisoner, she tried to form some plan for her safety.

Ruffina well knew that her husband would vent on her the disappointment these losses would cause him, for such was his amiable custom. What could she say, and what could she do? As she sat trying to bring her bewildered thoughts into order, troops of returning mouse-soldiers passed her door on their way to their homes. They were eagerly discussing the events of the battle; and by degrees it dawned on her dull senses that the fate of the conflict was decided, and that the frogs were defeated. And Rough wanted them to beat!

This thought, on top of the two other misfortunes, was the last straw to poor Ruffina's already heavy burden; and with a loud squeal of despair she rushed wildly away, intent only on escaping from the vengeance of the hard old miser; and never more was she heard from. Let us hope that she found a safe retreat, where, far from the old miser's influence, she may lead a more useful and better life.

We will not dwell on such an unpleasant subject as the rage of old Rough when he discovered the true state of affairs. With his propensity for thinking the worst of everybody, he concluded that his wife had run off with the stores she had obtained from the mice, and was living on them in some safe retreat luxuriously and happily. For a time he searched for his missing wife; but as day after day passed and no Ruffina appeared, he gave up the search.

These bitter disappointments did not tend to sweeten the temper of the old water-rat. Harder than ever did he press upon the little field-mice, who he considered owed him a bounty for living on his premises; more than ever did he exact from them, and many were the depredations he committed upon his neighbors of the woods and meadow.

He seemed to feel that he must make these innocent creatures responsible for his losses, and he was more dreaded than ever before.

"Each seized an ear of the old water-rat and held him fast with his strong beak."

CHAPTER XIX.

THE CHARM.

FOR a short time after her mishap on the battle-field, the Widow O'Warty was not in her usual good humor; but anger with one of her sanguine temperament is short lived; so before long the recollection of her wrongs faded away, and she regained her usual amiability.

The widow recalled the little brown frog's devotion to her at the time she was trampled upon by those thousands of feet, the recollection of which would always cause a cold shiver to run down her spine; she also remembered Brownella's frantic appeals to her for some sign that she still lived. All this was very soothing to the widow's feelings, and pleasant to dwell upon.

"An' the poor little thing has throuble enough of her own," said the widow to herself; "and it's mesilf that will aid her wid me own ixparience."

So, acting on this resolution, the widow sought the little brown frog, whom she found in a most dejected condition.

"It's mesilf that will be afther giving ye the good advice," said the good-natured widow, "for it's throuble of the same kind mesilf has had. It's the gineral ye want, me dear, ye can't conc'ale it."

"But he does n't want me," sobbed Brownella. "Once he could n't think enough of me; and now, although I try with all my might to please him, he takes every occasion to show how he despises me."

"That's jist it," replied the widow, seriously; and in her eagerness she hopped closer to the little brown frog. "Ye 're afther thrying too much to pl'ase him."

"How can that be?" asked Brownella; "is n't it natural to try to please those we like?"

"Av coorse it is," answered the widow; "but whin it 's more ixparience ye have, ye 'll find that the ither sex place no value on what they obtain without pains. What they have throuble to get is swate to thim."

"That seems strange," said Brownella. "I can't understand it; but I believe there is truth in what you say, for when I was rude and avoided him, Johnny the basso followed me everywhere."

"I tould ye so," replied the widow, triumphantly. "Now listen, till I relate the charrm I used with O'Warty. 'T was tould to me by an auld toad who was wan of the wisest craturs that iver lived, an' me own grandmither, askin' your pardin."

"Oh! do tell me," cried Brownella, eagerly. "I will do anything you say."

"Well," began the widow in a low and mysterious tone, "come near till me, for not to a living sowl have I iver afore bra'thed the charrm. It's a dark night ye must choose, whin neither moon nor stars are in the heavens; and whin ye approach the gineral's dwilling it's backwards ye must hop, and repate a charrm for the spirit of the woods:—

"'Spirit of the wood and dell,
Weave for me a fairy spell.

> Weave it strong, and weave it true,
> Grain of sand and drop of dew,
> Till it change my true love cold,
> Make him love me as of old.'

Thin whin ye have arrived forninst the dwilling, it's on the big toe of the right hind foot ye must sthand, an' wid the lift front foot (mind it's the *lift*), schrape up a thrifle of wather an' mud from the brook, an' throw it into the countenance of the gineral, rep'ating at the same time the following verse : —

> " ' Splisher, splasher, on one toe,
> Fairy spell o'er thee I throw.
> Be once more my own true love,
> Never more from me to rove.
> Splisher, splasher, on one toe,
> Fairy spell o'er thee I throw.'

If ye follow the directions the charrm will work; an' it's good luck I wishes ye," added the widow.

The little brown frog was profuse in her thanks for this valuable secret; and while she is waiting for a dark night to carry out the widow's instructions, we will follow the fortunes of other friends.

Little Fluff was so happy to be at home again that you may be sure he did not venture far away; and the fear that old Rough would seek him out and again imprison him was so strong, that for some time he imagined every rustling of the leaves, or sighing of the wind through the trees, to be the old miser coming in search of him. Gradually this feeling wore away, as day after day passed and old Rough did not appear, for Fluff was by nature bold and fearless.

For some time after the little squirrel's return, he and his brothers and sister did not venture off the tree beneath which their house stood; but by degrees they extended their playground, and raced over the neighboring trees, and hid among the rocks and stumps as before, taking care, however, not to go out of sight of home. It is hardly necessary to add that the old squirrels were as apprehensive as the younger ones, and since the dreadful day when Fluff was captured, never left their home unguarded, one always remaining to watch the little brood.

One warm, sunny afternoon, Squirrella sat in her doorway watching her little ones at play, thinking, as they raced about, that nowhere in the world could four other little squirrels be found with such bright eyes and such bushy tails. Up and down the tallest trees ran the happy little ones, jumping from bough to bough and from tree to tree, an occasional shrill chirrup from Squirrella warning them when the leap was too venturesome. Every thought of old Rough was forgotten by the frolicsome little creatures.

No one could have seen the innocent things sporting among the green leaves, or sitting on their little haunches, with their bright eyes shining with merriment and their bushy tails tilted over their striped backs, without thinking it would be difficult to find a more pleasing picture. Their brisk little chirrups, too, rang through the still woods in response to Squirrella's anxious calls; and timid little Bobtilla, with her young family about her, appeared at *her* door, and watched the frolics with great interest.

The excitement of the game was at its height, and Fluff's old venturesome spirit returned in full force, when a sudden impulse seized him to play a trick upon his companions; so he quickly slipped behind an old stump, where he waited, hoping soon to hear them calling to him, and laughing to himself all the while.

Fluff's absence was soon discovered, and loudly and eagerly did his name resound from the shrill voices of his playmates. This was great fun for the mischief-loving Fluff, who kept as still as a mouse, for fear his hiding-place would be discovered. Before long, however, he heard his mother's anxious call, and his merriment suddenly ceased; for at the sound of her distressed chirrup came the recollection of those dreary days of imprisonment in the old miser's dark den, and he hastened to assure her of his safety.

Fluff turned quickly to leave his hiding-place, and was about to utter a shrill cry of joy, when a dark shadow suddenly stood between him and the light, and the huge form and savage countenance of old Rough, with his long, sharp teeth and cruel black eyes was before him. The cry that was on Fluff's lips died away; and trembling from head to foot, he stood transfixed by the power of that cruel face.

"Aha!" squeaked the old rat, with a vicious grin. "I've caught you at last, have I? I haven't watched you for nothing all these days, I can tell you. I knew a heedless little fool like you would venture off before long. This time, my young friend, you will not get away so easily; old Rough is n't caught in the same trap twice, let me tell you. Come along, youngster!"

As the old rat approached, Fluff found voice, and his terrified cries rang through the silent wood, to be answered immediately by the agitated calls of his anxious family, and the fainter squeaks of Bobtilla's sympathetic children.

"Come along, I say," repeated old Rough, approaching the poor little squirrel.

"I won't!" screamed Fluff, boldly, for the answering cries came nearer and nearer, and what child does not believe that its mother's love is capable of saving it from the most powerful enemy? Fluff had the utmost confidence in his mother's power; and as her sharp cries came nearer and nearer, all his boldness returned, and he fearlessly faced his enemy.

"Go away, I tell you!" cried Fluff, valiantly, "or it will be the worse for you when my mother catches you! Here I am, Mother, right behind this old stump!"

"Little idiot!" snarled the old rat, "do you suppose a dozen such feeble creatures as your mother could intimidate me? Take that for your insolence in daring to oppose me!"

A piercing cry rang out as the old rat's sharp teeth penetrated Fluff's tender skin. The cry was immediately answered not only by the shrill tones of the squirrel family, and the distressed squeaks of Bobtilla, but by loud and harsh caws, and the two young crows lighted behind the old water-rat.

"Come, let the youngster alone!" demanded the elder of the crows. "Run home, Sonny," he added to Fluff.

"He'd better not," snarled old Rough, savagely, "he'd better not. As for you,

you impudent fellows, I advise you to mind your own business, and not interfere in what does n't concern you. Be off, I say!"

"We 're in no hurry, thank you," pertly answered the younger crow; "and as for attending to our own business, why, we have n't any on hand just now, and we have plenty of time to settle this matter, — so don't make yourself uneasy on our account. Come, Sonny, hurry home; your anxious mamma is looking for you."

Fluff needed no second bidding, but made a sudden rush by old Rough; the latter, however, was on the alert, and as the little squirrel was in the act of passing him, fastened his sharp, strong paws in Fluff's furry back. In another moment his long teeth would have buried themselves in Fluff's neck, had not the crows with a sudden movement come up behind, each seizing an ear of the old water-rat, and holding him fast with his strong beak.

At the same moment a flock of crows, attracted by the loud squeals of the old water-rat, flew down and fiercely attacked him, until the old miser wriggled himself free of his persecutors, and darting away, followed by the loudly-cawing crows, he slipped into an empty hole, where he secreted himself until the noisy band had departed. For once in their lives, the two young crows had made themselves useful.

This attempt to recapture the little squirrel was the absorbing topic of conversation among the inhabitants of the meadow and surrounding woods for some time to come. Indignation meetings were held, and many were the complaints made against the disagreeable old miser. The veteran Caw presided, for all felt great confidence in his sagacity if they did not in his honesty. These meetings grew more and more frequent as time wore on, and old Rough grew bolder after every success.

"This state of affairs must end," exclaimed an excited field-mouse. "We are tired of seeing our homes laid waste and our families houseless."

"*Houseless!*" cackled a motherly looking hen from Farmer Smith's poultry-yard; "is that the worst he has done to you? What would you say to having your children carried off before your very eyes, as he has done with mine?"

"And to be driven off when you are looking for food for your starving families?" squeaked Bobtilla's high voice.

"Talking and complaining will not mend the matter," croaked old Caw, who had listened with his head shrewdly turned to one side, taking in every word that had been uttered, "While you have been wasting time in talking, I've been making up my mind as to the best means of stopping it."

"How? Tell us how!" cried many eager voices.

"Since old Rough is so powerful, and carries things with such a high hand, meet him on his own ground, and confront him with an enemy who inspires him with the same terror he does you."

"Who is there he is afraid of?" asked the hen who had before made her complaint. "Who but Blinkeye is old Rough afraid of? And he is harmless by daylight, and Rough knows enough to keep out of his way at night."

"Have you forgotten the terrible fight Rough had with the weasel, who would have finished him, had not the farmer made his appearance when he did?" asked old Caw in his deepest croak.

"Oh!" cackled the hen, whose feathers stood up stiff with fright at the remembrance of that dreadful scene; "but old Rough has not ventured near the premises since, — he is too shrewd for that."

"The weasel can go to him, can't he?" croaked Caw.

"To be sure," assented all. "What a bright idea!"

"The weasel can make his headquarters under the wall, not far from old Rough's den, and take his own time about the matter," said Caw.

This easy solution of the question was so satisfactory that the spirits of the assembly rose suddenly, and all talked together in their excitement. The cackling of the hen, the shrill squeaking of the mice, and the croaks of the frogs and toads became so loud, that old Caw interposed.

"If you want to give old Rough notice of what is going to be done, keep on talking, that is all; but if you want the plan to succeed, make less noise about it," he said briefly.

Dead silence followed these words, the truth of which was so apparent; and soon the friends separated, returning quietly to their homes, secretly satisfied that old Caw was the wisest counsellor that ever lived, and would prove more than a match for even old Rough.

A few nights later, when the moon was hidden behind dark clouds, and a heavy fog had settled over the meadow, a lithe form might have been seen emerging from the direction of Farmer Smith's barn, and under cover of darkness gliding noiselessly toward old Rough's abode. After critically examining the stone wall that commanded a fine view of the old miser's den, it carefully selected a suitable opening, and in the same noiseless manner wriggled out of sight. It was the weasel, to whom old Caw had given instructions.

"He trembled with terror, and gave a shrill squeak of agony, as the long lithe body of his enemy the weasel came into view."

CHAPTER XX.

THE SPELL IS BROKEN.

ON the same night that the weasel took possession of his new quarters under the stone wall, a very different scene was being enacted in the neighborhood of the basso's dwelling. Ever since the Widow

O'Warty had given her instructions how to win back the affection of her former devoted friend, Brownella had watched eagerly for a night dark enough to carry out her design.

Never, it seemed to the impulsive Brownella, did the moon night after night shine brighter and more persistently, and in her impatience she began to think that it would always be thus. After long waiting, however, to her great joy one night she perceived light clouds drifting across the sky, for a few moments obscuring the brilliant moon; but there she was again, shining brighter than ever, and it seemed to Brownella's excited imagination as if her usually placid countenance wore a mocking expression, as if it would say, " I know you want me to keep out of sight, but I am determined not to," — and then on she sailed again into the clearer sky, lighting up every corner and cranny of the meadow.

However, Brownella was not doomed to

disappointment this time, for before long up came cloud after cloud; and as fast as the moon emerged from one, into another she went, until the whole heavens were suffused, and not even a star was visible.

Then did Brownella's heart beat fast with joy, and also with some fear; for now that the moment for which she had so long waited had arrived, many doubts arose in her mind. What if the charm should n't work? And what if she should neglect to follow in every respect the Widow O'Warty's instructions?

Agitated by her hopes and fears, Brownella hopped rapidly in the direction of the basso's dwelling. When within a short distance, she stopped and listened. All was still; the rich bass notes that were so musical to her ear were hushed; for the sensitive nature of the great singer sympathized with Mother Nature, and when her face was shrouded in darkness, his own spirits were affected likewise, and he remained at home silent and sad.

All the courage she possessed did Brownella summon to her aid, and carefully did she repeat to herself the lines on which her future happiness depended. When assured that she knew them accurately, Brownella turned her back upon the abode of the singer, and hopping backwards, repeated the following lines, —

> "Spirit of the wood and dell,
> Weave for me a fairy spell.
> Weave it strong, and weave it true,
> Grain of sand and drop of dew,
> Till it change my true love cold,
> Till he loves me as of old."

These lines did Brownella keep repeating until she reached the brook that flowed in front of the basso's dwelling, and where he was now sitting; then, approaching him, and standing on the big toe of her right hind foot, with the left fore foot she scraped up some of the mud and water from the stream, and threw it into the face of the astonished basso, saying,—

> "Splisher, splasher, on one toe,
> Fairy spell o'er thee I throw.
> Be once more my own true love,
> Never more from me to rove.
> Splisher, splasher, on one toe,
> Fairy spell o'er thee I throw."

This verse was answered by a resounding "a-hung!" uttered in the deepest and tenderest tones of the basso-profundo's voice, and Brownella knew that the charm had done its work, and that the singer's heart was hers once more.

Leaving this happy pair, we will return to other scenes.

Old Rough grew more miserly and ill-natured day by day. Everybody avoided him, and he lived alone in his den, slinking around by himself, adding constantly to the stores he had collected, and tyrannizing over all with whom he came in contact. His countenance, never agreeable, became every day more repulsive; his eyes seemed to grow smaller and nearer together, and his nose longer and sharper, while his wrinkled lips receded from the long, sharp teeth.

Not a living creature approached the old miser, and he crouched in his den, gloating over the vast wealth he possessed, and concocting plans for gaining more. No longing for the companionship of his fellow creatures ever stole over him in his solitude, and still less a regret that he had done nothing to gain the respect and affection of any of his neighbors. Not even a desire that Ruffina, who had served him so faithfully, would return, did the sordid old fellow feel; his only wish in regard to her was that he might obtain possession of the provisions he supposed her to have carried off, and also to wreak vengeance on her for his various disappointments.

One night old Rough was out on one of

his foraging expeditions, for he always chose darkness for his depredations. A raw east wind was blowing, and a drizzling rain was falling. Not a star was to be seen, and only a dark mass against the sky showed in which direction the woods lay. This was just the weather the old water-rat enjoyed, and he was in particularly good spirits, for he had the day before overheard a conversation between the two young crows, in which they spoke of some very rare morsels they had concealed under a certain stone in the woods. So accurately did they describe the spot that Rough could have gone to it blindfolded; and he chuckled to himself with satisfaction as he thought how shrewd he was, and how inexperienced the young crows were.

Shrewd as was the old water-rat, he little knew that the crows were acting under the advice of one much shrewder and slyer than he, — none other than the old crow Caw, —

and that this conversation was merely a trap, into which he readily fell.

"The young thieves! I should like to watch their countenances when they find that the treasure they hid with such care has been discovered," squeaked the old rat to himself, as he slid over the meadow toward the wood. "This will help pay for the trick they played me in leading me into that rascally weasel's hole; but I 've a nice little plan of my own, youngsters, to make us even on that score. You 'll find it out in due time."

Thus communing with himself, old Rough proceeded on his way, often sitting upright and looking about him to see if all were safe, and frequently poking his long nose about, in hope of finding something that he could turn to account. In this manner he reached the wood, where the darkness was even denser than outside; but this was all the better for his purposes, and his spirits rose as he neared his destination.

On by the homes of the squirrels and Bobtilla, and of many other little inhabitants of the forest, did the old rat go, and at his approach many a mouse out in search of food ran trembling into its hole, hardly daring to breathe, until the dreadful figure had passed. Only the bats flitted fearlessly between the dense forest trees; but they had no terrors for him.

At last the old rat paused, and poked his long nose anxiously about. Had he lost his way,—he who knew every bit of woodland and meadow about? Or had those thievish young crows deceived him? This last thought was not an agreeable one, and made his small black eyes twinkle with malice, and his long teeth snap viciously together.

As he squatted on his haunches, glancing through the darkness for some landmark, a slight rustling of leaves attracted his atten-tion. "Some hedgehog returning from

Farmer Smith's poultry-yard, or a clumsy woodchuck," muttered old Rough.

He was mistaken; it was neither of the two; he trembled with terror, and gave a shrill squeak of agony, as the long lithe body of his enemy the weasel came into view.

The next day there was great rejoicing in the meadow and woods. The crickets chirped their loudest; the katydids and locusts sang shriller than ever before; the little mice ran squeaking about fearlessly in the tall grass; the squirrels ran heedlessly over walls and trees, loudly chirruping their joy, — all small creatures were doing their best to express their delight that old Rough the miser would no longer persecute them, — for the weasel had at last vanquished the dreaded tyrant, and no more would they fear him. In the midst of this rejoicing, a flock of crows perched on the tree that grew behind old Rough's former abode, and old Caw repeated with great solemnity, —

    "'War and strife, grief and woe,
       Follow you where 'er you go.
       Never more shall you know rest
       For weary feet and aching breast,
       Till body round and lithe and long
       Shall vanquish body thick and strong.
       Then shall dawn a day of peace,
       Then shall strife and sorrow cease.'

"Friends," added old Caw, "the spell that has hung over the inhabitants of this meadow and wood for so long a time is now broken. The 'body round and lithe and long' *has* at last 'vanquished body thick and strong,' and no more need you dread the old miser's power."

That evening when the moon rose over the woodland, and shone down on the meadow, a gay throng came from bog and stream and wood. Choruses of frogs and crickets and locusts filled the air, while the little mice squeaked an accompaniment; hundreds of lively bats flitted in and out, and fireflies and glow-worms lighted up the gay scene; for old Rough the miser had disappeared forever, and the spell that had for so long hung over them was at last broken.

THE END.

www.ingramcontent.com/pod-product-compliance
Lightning Source LLC
Chambersburg PA
CBHW031024120726

47905CB00007B/2038